I0664087

MR. GOODNIGHT

By
David Broussard

MR. GOODNIGHT

Copyright © 2011 by David Broussard

All Rights reserved. No part of this book may be reproduced or transmitted in any form or by any means without written permission of the author.

ISBN-13: 978-0615474502

I dedicate this book to all the beautiful women in the world that I have had the pleasure of meeting. Also, those women who I have not had the pleasure of meeting.

For it is your true beauty, that naturally inspires me.

Acknowledgments

I'd like to thank my loving Mom and Dad for all of there support, love and understanding. My kids, David Jr., Branden, Brittan and James for all there love and laughter throughout the years. My older brother and sister, Gregory and Christina for there love and guidance. I want to thank all my good friends for there great friendship and my co-workers for letting me have so many fond memories and a great time at work. I would also like to thank Prince for the great inspiration of the title.

Table of Contents

Chapter One

I look at my cell phone and push the favorite's button. I see a name that is very familiar to me so I push her name and the phone quickly dials her number.

"Ring, ring, ring", and "Hello" she says, Silence fills the air.

"Hello, I said. Is anyone there"? She says. I answer in a deep voice. "It is me, my darling. What are you doing"?

"Oh, nothing much". She answers.

"So what do you have on darling"? I reply. She says, "I have on a soft, black silky baby doll nighty".

"Sounds really sexy, are you alone"? I say.

"Yes I am, but I'm tired and I want to go to sleep. So I'll talk to you later o.k."

I answer, "O.K. I'll talk to you later. Bye for now."

I hang up the phone and start to think about all the good times we had together. I think about her touch. I think about the way she smells and what I really wanted to do that night.

After about ten minutes, I call her back and tell her that I am coming over, I'll be right there. I hang up before she could say anything. I grab some smell good out of the bathroom and give myself a couple of splashes.

I grab my keys and head down the stairs to my whip. Place the key in the lock and unlock the car. Put it in the ignition and start the car up. I headed down the street to her place and all I thought about was her on the way.

When I got to her place I parked, and before I got out of the car I started thinking about what was I doing. Was I really going to do this? Was I out of my mind or what? I changed the song on the CD player to Mr. Goodnight and elevated myself into my player groove.

I was ready now so I turned the car off and got out. Shrugged my shoulders and started up the walkway. I got to the door and rung the door bell. Ding Dong. I heard a voice say "who is it"?

I answer, "It is me darling". She says "Mr. Goodnight, I know it's not you".

She opens the door and looks me in the eyes. I say "Yes, it's me baby. I had to see you". She says "you shouldn't have come here".

I tell her I know, but I wanted to see you baby. She opens the door all the way and says are you coming in or what. I walk into the room and grab her hand on the way in closing the door behind me. I force her against the wall and she says "what are you doing"? But before she could say anything else, I grab her on both of her arms and push her against the wall.

Kissing her madly and passionately I knew what she really wanted. She had been playing hard to get for months and I knew really, what we both wanted.

She just didn't want to seem to be easy.

As I kissed her I could hear her say the yes sounds and I knew that I was going to wear it out.

I went for her neck and she dared not push me away. I kissed her with my tongue and licked both her lips top and bottom. She pulled me closer to her and I new even more then that I had her were I wanted her.

I grabbed her hand and placed it on my penis. Hard and erect it was, as she rubbed it slowly and gently. I went for the twins. Yes, the twins I think to myself.

I had been wanting the twins for so long and finally I had my chance.

I touched one of them so slow that I was almost scared to let go. It seemed like the nipple got hard as I touched it or was it just my imagination. I bent down to lick it because I knew that it was going to taste so right. I licked the nipple slowly and took it all the way out of her black nighty. Oh the taste of her nipple with all the firmness and attention that I expected. One down, and one to go.

I look at the other tit and blamm. I take the other out and taste it. It's good, and very delicious. Firm to the tip, and juicy on the outside. Yummy yum.

Hey, wait a minute. This is the girl that wouldn't give me the time of day, and I had to put so much time into. I had to call her every day and night. I had to call her on my break and even while I was in the restroom sometimes. She is so bad that I had to have some of her.

I kiss her some more and now its time for the cookie. I grab her and start toward the bed room. She says no, but I really know that she means yes. Yes its time for Mr. Goodnight.

I got you now. So I push her onto the bed that I backed her up against. I climb on top of her, and madly start kissing her again on the mouth and neck. I kiss her on her eye lids. I kiss her on the lips. She starts to unbuckle my pants and grab at my dick.

Now she is rubbing me as if she wanted nothing else but me at that moment. I pull off her gown and start for the panties.

She tells me we shouldn't be doing this and I agree, but before she could stop me I was already touching her soft and wet coochy.

Warm and wet it was ready for me to do what ever I wanted to. So I did.

I went down slowly licking her up and down. I licked around the clit and barley licked inside of her. She was moaning and groaning for more. I couldn't take it. She was driving me crazy as well as I was driving her crazy. I fingered her just a little bit and she made a sound like she had cum instantly.

I know that she didn't cum yet I thought to myself. She was so wet now. I barley put my finger inside her and she was going crazy.

I used the wetness of her pussy and put some on her anal hole. She again made a sound like she had cum and wanted more and more.

She told me that she had never felt like this and that I had shown her a new spot. So I fingered her with just the tip of my finger. She begged for more, so I gave her more, but not to put my entire finger inside of her.

"I have to have you inside me" she said. "I want you now". She told me twice.

So I reached for a condom and she said. "I don't use those. You don't have to worry".

I told her that I have not had sex without one on for so long that I don't know what if feels like without it.

She reassured me that she was very clean and that she had not had sex for 4 years. I thought about it for a moment and said "what the hell".

I tossed the rubber and started for the coochy without it. What was I thinking? I know better than this. But I wanted her so bad and she wanted me too. I was so hard that I knew why they call it penitentiary steel.

I climbed on top of her, ready for placement. Before I rubbed it on the entrance to her vagina, I said a quick prayer.

"Please protect me". And I entered her wet, warm, hairy vagina.

"Oh", as I just put the head of my penis inside her. It was very hot like fire. And I had not had that feeling since I don't know how long.

We both moaned and groaned as we said the same words. "Ooohhh". "Yhea baby". "Yhea".

She grabbed me so tight I knew that she had not had something inside her for quite awhile. She was so damn tight, and I was so large, that I knew that I wasn't going to last very long.

So after about two dozen humps, I had to do something fast. I pulled out and told her to wait a minute. I said, "I want to taste how sweet it is baby".

She jumped up and pushed me down and started to kiss me on my neck. She started on my chess and then down to my stomach. I knew exactly where she was going with this. And yes before I could say stop she had my dick in her hands and wrapped her lips around my head.

Licking me at first, then she put my head inside her mouth. It felt so warm and good; I started to wonder if I was going to get sprung or was she already sprung. Were we both going to be sprung or was it going to be just sex for the both of us.

She started to go all the way down and deep throat me. I said to myself she knows what she's doing.

"Damn baby, that's feels good" I told her out loud. She looked at me and said,

"You like that daddy". "MMMM, you know it baby", I answered.

She tightened up around my penis with her hand as if she wanted to make all the blood go to the top of my dick head. Then she licked it with the tip of her tongue. She did this over and over till I was moaning and groaning and saying things I never said to any women before.

"Yes baby, you go girl".

"That's your dick".

"Make me cum".

"You want daddy to cum don't you".

I was going crazy and she was definitely making me her slave. I never thought I would be someone's sex slave. But I was hers for the taking. I told her that I have to have you. "I want you now".

She insisted that I cum in her mouth and said it in a very giving way.

"I want you to cum in my mouth", she said three times and I pulled back and held back as long as I could, making sure that I didn't cum in her mouth yet.

After about 10 minutes of head she started to let down and I knew that it was my time now. She had sharpened my tool to perfection. And now it was time to put her to sleep.

I told her "lay back baby. It's my turn". Her pussy was so wet that I knew she loved sucking dick. Not to mention she was on it for ten minutes.

She laid back and opened her legs. I looked at the hairy, wet monkey and moved slowly toward her.

As I got closer and closer, I said, "Are you ready for Mr. Goodnight". She smiled and said "Yes, come on daddy". I loved it when she calls me daddy.

I placed the head inside her and she grabbed me tightly. Pushing myself in slowly but surely, she sounded like a record.

"Ooooohhhhhh", she moaned.

I stopped pushing inside of her and pulled out some. I pushed in some more and this time all the way in. she screamed "wait baby".

I told her no baby, your going to enjoy this.

I played with the pussy by just putting the head in. In and out repeatedly, about three times and then pushing it all the way in. Slowly I go all the way in and out.

Out and in some more, then a little faster. Stopping after about ten humps, starting over and over. This was driving her crazy and I think she had cum about three times. I couldn't tell for sure but at times she would grab me, squeeze me and start to tremble.

She was already making the yes sounds and saying my name, so I wasn't for sure when she came exactly. But then I started what I call the mercy hump.

That's when I go a little faster than usual and bang on the pussy, as if I was trying to beat it up.

Hump, hump, hump, bang…. Hump, hump, hump, bang. I know that I can't hurt any pussy cuz it stretches and stretches, but this is the for sure go getter. Every time I banged on it she would scream. "Oh, yes, yes, Oh, yes, yes Oh". Then she started the Ooooohhhh shit and you know what that means.

She was definitely Cuming, so I kept it going. Mercy hump….. Mercy hump….. mercy hump. I can't keep this up long because of all the sounds and friction.

I start making sounds that I never made before and she started making sounds that I never heard before. She could feel me going to explode inside her. And I ask her the big question.

"Do, you want me to cum inside you"?

She says, "Yesssss".

I ask her again.

"Do you want me to cum inside you baby"?

She said, "Yes baby, yes. Cum inside me".

What I was feeling at that moment and what she was feeling at that moment was definitely some way out shit because I bust a big fat nut inside of her and it seemed like we both were screaming at the top of our lungs. I know the whole street had to hear us but I didn't feel any shame. I was Mr. Goodnight.

As we both came together and enjoyed the feeling of ecstasy at that moment. I started to rub her every so gently.

Slowly grinding her, and still hard inside of her. I didn't want to pull out.

I rubbed her some more and rubbed her gently till she calmed down. I slowly and gently rubbed her head, shoulders, neck, titties, ass, legs and everything in between.

We both moaned and groaned till we were at a mmmmm, mmmmm, good.

All we both could say was "Baby, oh Baby".

As I pulled out and pushed away from her, she jumped up and said wait here.

She went into the bathroom and turned on the hot water. She returned with a warm towel and started to wipe me off.

I thought to myself this is a really nice woman. The warmth of the towel felt so good to me. She wiped so slow and careful as if she could understand that my penis is so sensitive after I cum.

She looked at me and said, "It's not going down". I looked at her and laughed.

"You did that" I told her.

"That's your dick. You made it that way. Your pussy shouldn't have been so good". She looked at me and laughed.

She asked me if she could put it back into her mouth. I said "are you crazy"?

She said "No. Please let me put it in my mouth".   Before I could say no she had it back in her mouth. And it was on again.

It felt so good and I was still hard. I told her to just be careful baby. It's very sensitive. She said o.k. and licked it up and down just putting the head into her mouth. Man, this felt good but I knew where it was going. She was trying to put me asleep. She wanted me to cum again. And maybe spend the night.

I told her after about 5 minutes that I had to go. I had to get up early and had a very important meeting.

She agreed that I could leave but made me promise that I would come back over later. So I promised and headed for the shower.

As I was taking a shower, I thought about what we had done. How great it was and how I had waited so long for this. I almost yelled in the shower as if I had scored a touchdown. Clinching my fist and pounding the other, "Yes".

After my shower, I came out of the bathroom and she was sitting in a chair crying.

"Baby, what's wrong? She looked at me and said, "I think I'm on love". I thought about my next words and looked her right in the eyes and said.

"Aaww, baby. I love you more".

Big mistake, never say the "I love you" words unless you mean it.

When I saw her crying I never thought that this would lead to something terrible. I just thought that she was really emotional and she was in love.

I got dressed and kissed her before I left out the door as she was in the shower, but not before I told her I had to leave.

Down the steps I went, on a high that was right. I got to my ride and unlocked the door.

As I got in my whip, I thought man that was some good sex. Of course on my way home, she called me and I had to tell her after a few minutes that I would call her later and that I really had a great time with her.

I could tell she didn't want to let me get off the phone. I thought all the way home about her. Was this going to be the lady in my life? Was she going to be my one and only? Maybe even my wife.

Nope. Not for Mr. Goodnight.

She was just a woman that had crossed my path. A victim for the taking. Someone that had given me such a hard time that I had to punish her.

She thought that she was untouchable and I had to prove her wrong.

No woman is untouchable. Call it head games or what ever you want, but no woman is untouchable.

I got home and checked my messages and had a few from other ladies that just wanted to say goodnight. I laughed, no man or woman really just wants to say goodnight at the booty call hours. Yep, I said it.

The booty call hours are midnight to five in the morning. Why is it called the booty call hours? Because if the phone rings at that time it is most definitely a booty call no matter what is said on the phone. It leads to getting some booty.

Nothing is open at that time but motels and legs. Women laugh about this but they know that it is very true. They may seam to not want to open there legs, but if you get to touch there legs at these hours of the night. They will open with toes pointed to the sealing, and the cookie saying come to me, and singing I'm yours.

I grab me something out of the fridge and get me some cranberry juice before I jump onto the bed. I look at the sealing in my room and then look over to my life size picture on the wall and say "have a sweet dream Mr. Goodnight".

Chapter Two

I wake up the next morning and jump into the shower. As I brush my teeth looking in the mirror, I'm feeling alive with happiness.

Turned up the music on my radio and started to dance. Thinking of the night before, I had the feeling of accomplishment.

I had captured another prey for the trophy room. Ms. Sexy was mine for the taking and I took her. It took me 3 months to do it, but never the less I did it. And I was damn proud of it.

This lady was fine as wine and everyone knew it. I like to say that when women are fine that they remind me of the sun setting over a water fall in the spring time.

It makes them laugh and they think that it's cute. I love to call them darling with a heavy accent.

"Hello darling, how var you"? In a heavy foreign accent.

Knowing that I am not French or Russian but they love it anyway.

I try to be lots of fun because that's all they want most of the time. They just want to have some fun.

I grab my sax on the way out of the door. I never leave home without it.

On the way to work my cell phone rings. It's another victim that I'm working on. This one is a little different. She is tall, thick, and very cute and has lots of money too. She seems to be very intelligent. But I know that I can break her if given the time.

She drives a BMW and lives up in the hills. But she is crazy about me and she likes to play hard to get. So I play along with her. She loves oldies and I do too, so I invite her to some of my shows and blow some oldies on my sax for her. She loves it. But I just don't know what it is that's going to break her into giving me the cookie.

She has only kissed me twice and it was without the tongue. That must be it. I have to kiss her with my tongue. If she tongue kisses me I will have her where I want her.

So I have to plan it right. It has to be at the right moment and the right place, so I can move in for the kill.

Hey baby, what's happening with you? She says "nothing much, just wanted to say hello to you".

So I say "Hello Darling, how var you?" in my foreign voice. She loves it and laughs at me.

She says that we must get together and I agree. So I tell her that I can see her tonight after practice. She agrees.

"So it's a plan. I'll see you about 10 pm tonight".

She says o.k. and tells me to have a good day. I tell her bye bye for now and hang up the phone.

It's all falling into place. Some women can tell if you've had sex because of how thick your sperm is, if you get into that.

I will definitely were a condom with this women because she is not of this kind where I would want to have a baby with or is trustworthy. She doesn't make me laugh that much and I would dare not eat her coochie.

Some ladies are clean and every thing but I just wouldn't eat there cookie. If you know what I mean, just wouldn't do it.

I get to work and head for my desk. There's a note on my desk that says "I really had a nice time" with a happy face on it, but no name.

This is strange because I don't know who it could be. I try not to shit were I have to eat. That is a golden rule that I live by. Don't screw ladies at the job. Things can really end up pretty shitty. But of course not every one follows the rules. And of course I had to make a few exceptions.

Now I remember. It's all coming back to me. It must be from the pretty lady on the 6 floor. We had such a great time together. Yes, it has to be her. But that was two weeks ago. I guess she wants some more of Mr. Goodnight. I smiled and patted myself on the back.

Back to the crazy lady that I had to deal with at work. What a lesson learned.

It started out just fine as all relationships do. We were both happy and enjoying each other. Once we had sex everything started to change. She started getting jealous bossy. I don't like bossy ladies. It's just not me.

Now when were in bed and a woman wants to take control and start telling me how she wants it, that's totally different? But when a woman wants you to call at a certain time and be at a certain place at a certain time, it's very hard to be punctual if you're a busy man like me.

I have a lot on my plate because I like to have fun and enjoy life. I am into jazz and my saxophone so I am around lots of pretty ladies all the time.

She could not accept this. She thought that I was screwing every one around me.

Now some of the ladies around me, I have screwed before. But we are all adults and what was then was then and what is now is now. You know what I mean. I liked what I saw and they liked what they saw so we both came to a mutual agreement. We had sex and it was over. No strings attached. I went on with my life and they went on with theirs.

But she couldn't understand this. She was very jealous and wanted to fight other ladies. Even if they had never have had sex with me and was just friendly.

Boy did I make a big mistake getting involved with her. I came home a few times and found her waiting for me. "What are you doing here"? I would ask her. She said that she wanted to see me. But I know that she was trying to catch me with another girl.

My game is too good for shit like that. No lady has ever caught me with another lady if she was mine at that time.

My relationships really don't last that long because I guess I get board with ladies. I know that I want something and I go get it. Some give good head; some don't give head at all.

Some let you have a little anal sex. Some are very afraid of that. They say it's too painful.

Some are just as freaky as you want them to be but they are not the kind that you want someone to see you with if you know what I mean.

On the cute scale they are a 2 to 4 out of 10. They will just get a creep move in the middle of the night. And I will never be seen in public with them. I do have a reputation to uphold ya know.

So at my lunch time I grab a tuna sandwich and some ginseng to give me some strength for later.

I don't like to take the pills that some swear by. They say that they work wonders and get you hard as a rock. But I don't trust them. They also eat your liver and kidneys. Not for me. All natural is the way to go. Ginseng baby, ginseng tea.

I also went to the fish market after work and got me some oysters. Yhep, good old oysters make me hard as a rock and the ladies love it when mans penis is hard as a rock.

It gives them a scenes of yes I am very sexy, cuz this dude is hard as a rock. He wants me, he wants me so bad. Not to mention that they think you haven't had sex in a while with a hard on like that.

After I left the fish market I headed to practice to blow with some friends. Sax is my first love and I will always love her. I was playing the sax before I was chasing girls. Well not really, but I had not had sex yet. So the sax is my first love.

I started chasing girls in 4th grade. I had to stand on her feet to kiss her because she was taller than me. I got caught in the girls' bathroom grinding and kissing. I thought that was sex in the forth grade.

What a life. I even had a few guys start fights with me because they thought I was trying to take there girl.

When I got to rehearsal, they were warming up. But the keyboard player was not there yet.

"Hey guys, what it do"?

"Hey Good, what's happenin? You ready to jam"? They answered. "Yhea, we gone shoot up the house tonight".

"So where is Keys"? I asked.

"He called and said the he was going to be a little late, he had to pick up a friend".

"Yhea, he said that he was bringing a singer that likes to sing jazz".

"Cool".

So I pulled out my horn and put it together. Placed the reed on the mouthpiece, and tightened up the ligature. Placed the mouthpiece on the neck and started to tune my axe.

After tuning my horn, I started to play some scales just to warm up and then I started playing "the closer I get to you".

One of the guys jumped up and said "Hey, what's that you're playin"?

I told him it was "the closer I get to you".

He said "Man, that sounds nice. We should play that song". I told him that it was a song that I was working on. And I was possibly going to put it on my new album.

He got really excited about it and said that I had to let him play on that track. I told him that he definitely was going to play on the track with me on this song.

So we played around with it and he seamed to learn it really quick. The drummer kind of picked it right up. I just told him to do his thing.

I didn't really know what I wanted yet. I knew I didn't want it like the original song. I wanted something a little different. I had to keep it a ballad, just wanted it to be a little different.

So the keyboard player comes in and he has a guest.

"Hey man, what's good"?

"What's happenin"?

"How you doin"? Everyone greets him and his guest.

He walks in with some very attractive lady and everyone is looking at her because she is so stunning. This girl is tall, sexy and has a very nice ass and big tits.

Keys introduces her,

"Hey guys, this is Sexy. Sexy these are the fellas". Everyone says at the same time "Hey Sexy". She has her eyes on me and I am locked on her.

"Sexy wants to sing with us on some of the tunes". I said, "So is this an audition or something like that". The keyboardist says "No, I auditioned her at my place and she passed with flying colors". I say to him, "Very good sir".

So he sets up his keyboard and plugs it in and starts to play some chords. The bass player says "Hey man, we been working on some new material that Good wants to put on his album".

"Oh yhea", says the keyboardist.

"What does it sound like".

"Its cool man, play some of it for him Good". I start to play a little. He cuts right in and says "the closer I get to you. Yhea, you know it. He says "Man keep it goin".

The keyboardist feels the groove and finds his chords. In a matter of minutes we were playing the tune really nicely and the singer started to sing something but it was not like the song.

So I tried to teach her the song and ended up writing the words down with her and told her to just follow behind me a little.

It really didn't fit like I wanted it too so I suggested that we try something else. I told her that she should go ahead and do what ever she felt. She had a green light to do what ever.

She looked at me and gave me the biggest smile. It was so big that it lit up the place. She had an amazing voice and I wanted her to really show off her talent. I told her to just join in when ever she felt like it.

We kicked off the song and I started playing the lead. She joined right in with a jazzy scat that sounded really nice. As a matter of fact it sounded so nice that I had to stop the song and give her credit on how good she was sounding.

I told her. "Sexy, that is the shit and I hope that you can remember what you're doing because that is the shit.

She laughs at me and says I can remember it. Damn Sexy, you do your thing girl. She looks at me with a shimmer in her eye and gives me a wink. And I wink back.

I kick off the song again and man it really is sounding great. It was missing a lot of synthesizer strings but I know we could get that later.

After about two more times doing the song I said I have to record this just like this so we don't forget what it wounds like.

I go out to my car to get my recorder and Sexy comes out behind me.

"Good, is that your name"?

"Yhea Sexy, that's my name. It stands for Mr. Goodnight". She laughs and says "That's different".

"Mr. Goodnight huh".

I open the trunk and get the recorder out of a bag that I have. She says to me, "I really love your sax playin. Your sound is so smooth and sexy".

I tell her thank you. She says, "We should play together more often. I think we should exchange numbers". I look at her as I close the trunk and say "Do you think Keys would be alright with that"?

She says "Keys is only a friend and why shouldn't he be alright with it. I am a single lady".

That was my cue. I looked at her smiled and said "Me too".

As we entered back into the hall, she took her phone out as if she wanted Keys to see her putting my number in her phone.

"What's your number"? She says. I give her my number and she puts it into her phone and Keys is looking like this bitch aint shit. At that moment I know he had been thinking about hittin it.

But a player is a player. So I give her my number and take out my phone and get hers. Keys knows how it is. We are peter in-laws.

We have had the same girl before and even once we had one at the same time together. Bitches aint shit but hoes and tricks.

All during the rehearsal, I was thinking about her and could not help myself. I would look at her during solos and lead parts all night. She would give me a wink a few times when I hit high notes.

After the rehearsal I was packing up and I told Keys that I think she wanted me to hit while she was gone into the bathroom. He agreed and gave me his approval to hit. So when she came out I asked her if she had any plans for the rest of the night.

"No, I don't". She replied.

"Would you like to get a cup of coffee"? I said.

"How about some tea, I don't drink coffee". She said.

"Sure thing darling", In my foreign voice as I smiled at her.

She smiled back and we walked toward my whip.

I open the car door for her and tapped her on her butt while she got into the car.

After she sits down. She looks at me and I immediately tell her,

"Did I just do that, I am so sorry darling" in my foreign voice.

"Watch your knee", as I close the door.

I walk around to the other side open the door and get in. I tell her to buckle her seat belt and fasten mine.

"So Sexy, I know a great place by my place that has great tea. They have green, grey earl and even a cranberry tea. Those are my favorites but they have more to choose from". She says "That's fine, were ever you want to take me".

I start up the car and head for the coffee shop. I turn up the music as some of my favorite music is playing. Will Downing, Break up to make up.

She says "That song is very nice. I love Will".

I agreed, "me too. But I don't like his new album. It sounds like he's doing a stage play. Maybe he's going toward the stage or something".

She says "o.k.", and bobs her head up and down.

On the hook she grabs my hand and sings along with the hook.

"Break up to make up, that's all we do. First you love me, then you hate me. That's a game for fools…."

I tell her "Wow, your voice is such an addictive sound". She smiles and puts my hand on her leg. Her leg is so soft; I rub on it and gently squeeze it. She has on a short skirt, so I can feel her tender skin. I try not to go up to high as I rub on her leg but go up just enough to let her know that I am interested in her sexiness.

Her thighs are so soft and silky I get a hard on just thinking about how it could be inside her. I try to adjust myself in the drivers' seat so my hard on doesn't feel uncomfortable and she looks down at my zipper area.

She says "I see someone is a little excited".

I tell her I couldn't help it and blame it on her. "You are so sexy and your skin is so soft I could not help but to fantasize about you".

Her eye brows go up and she smiles and says "fantasize! What did you fantasize"?

I say "I can't tell you, it wouldn't be a fantasy". She laughs and so do I.

"So how far from the coffee shop do you live", she says.

"I live just up ahead darling". I answer in my foreign voice.

"Would you like to see my place", I ask her and she says "sure I would".

I hit a corner and drive right for the Bat Cave.

"I know I have some tea. I will make you some". She says "Sure you will" and laughs as she grabs my penis. Mmmmm, she hums.

"Do you have a girl friend"? She says. Immediately I say "No I don't". As I pull up to park in the back of my place she bends over and unzips my zipper. She pulls out my dick and stats sucking on it. I let the seat back and say "Oh Shit, That feels good".

She asks me "Do you like that"? I tell her "Yes, I do. I like that very much". I then say we have to go inside. I can't believe this is happening.

She says, "yes you can and it is definitely happening.

She gets up off the dick and I let my seat up after I zip up my zipper.

"Come on baby lets go inside". I get out and walk around to open her door for her. Close and lock my doors then grab her hand and walk to my door as I can't wait to get inside.

As we enter the door, she says "Wow, your place is very nice. I can tell you love music and you're a musician. You have music stuff everywhere".

I grab her from behind so she could feel me on her ass. I was really hard and wanted her really bad.

I unzipped her skirt and pulled it down. Turned her around and started to kiss her as I backed her against the wall.

Touching her all over her body I move in for the twins. Unbuttoning her top, I open her blouse. Grab one of the twins and squeeze it while kissing her on the neck. She makes an mmmm sound. I try to unfasten her bra as I start to kiss her on the chest area. The bra comes undone and I pull it off.

The twins are looking at me right in the eyes. I tell her that she has the most beautiful breast that I have ever seen. I grab one of them ever so gently and start to kiss it. I then lick on it and play with the nipple with the tip of my tongue. Sucking and kissing back and forth each of the twins so that one doesn't get jealous as she gets wound up.

I pull off her panties and drop them on the floor. Pick her up and start for the bed. She is kissing me and tells me. "Take me, I'm yours".

I throw her on the bed and look at her like she is my prey. I start to climb on top of her. I kiss her stomach, navel, breast and then neck.

I reach over to the drawer for some protection and pull out some rubbers. She grabs one and says let me put it on as she tears open the package. Pulls out the rubber and puts it in her mouth.

She pushes me over and goes down on me again. Putting the rubber on while it is in her mouth and giving me head at the same time. I think to myself, wow she's a pro. Once the rubber is on the head, she pushes it down my penis and it feels so good.

She has sharpened the tool and now it was time to put in some work. I tell her to lie down. She gets up and lays back. I climb on top of her and gently place the head inside her but not before rubbing the outside of her vagina with the head of my penis.

She is wet and I am hard as steel. Those oysters really work wonders. As I enter inside her she sighs and says "ooohhh yes".

"Yes", I say back. Slowly starting our ride together she grinds back at me. At that moment I knew she wanted to get her nut too. She grabs my ass and I grab hers. We both make sounds of passion.

"Yes, ooh, yes, oohh".

The pussy is so wet and tight. I suck on her tah tahs and she starts to get loader.

"Oh, baby, Oh, baby". I answer back, "Yes baby, ooooh".

This feels so good. She says, "You like that". I say "yes baby. I love it".

She says "That's your pussy baby. Get it. Get it. Ooww, ooh, ooh, ooh", she screams as I start my mercy humps.

Hump, hump, bang. Hump, hump, bang. She screams, "I'm Cuming. I'm Cuming. Baby, baby, oooooohhhhh. Don't stop, don't stop".

At that moment I could not help myself and started to almost cum. So I started to bang the pussy as hard as I could.

She started screaming "Good, Good, Goooooood, Gooooood."

I bust a good fat nut inside her and give a few mercy humps as I scream her name.

"Oh, Sexy, Sexy you mutha fucka". She grabs my ass as pulls me close to not let go and grinds me as if she wants to be in control. She got me screaming like a baby.

"Oh, shit. Baby. Baby". She says the same.

"Baby, Baby". I asked her if she came and she said as if you didn't know laughing.

I start signing together baby, together baby. She laughs and we both lay there in ecstasy. I caress her and she rubs on me. I think to myself I can't believe this happened.

I just met this woman. But that's the life of Mr. Goodnight.

She starts grinding on me some more and says he is still hard. She rolls me over and gets off me. Goes into the bathroom and brings back a warm towel. Pulls the rubber off and wipes me off with the warm towel.

"Thank you baby, that feels good". She goes back into the bathroom and washes the towel out. Brings it back and wipes me off again and says "you must have really liked it because you're not getting soft.

She puts the towel down and grabs my dick. Bends down and says "he loves me".

She starts to lick it again and I tell her "Please baby it's so sensitive right now".

She says "o.k. I'll be gentle".

She licks it up and down the shaft and licks my balls. I tell her "ooohh that feels good".

It didn't take long because I was already hard but she had me ready to go again for round two. I tell her "Let's get ready to rumble".

I jump up and slap her on the ass and say, "Come her baby".

I grab another rubber and tell her to bend over, "Let me hit it from the back. Doggy Style".

She smiles and starts to assume the position. I give a couple of barks and slap her on the ass. She says "Oooh. Get it daddy".

I put the rubber on and tell her "Now I'm really going to satisfy you baby". She says "Get it daddy, get it".

I rub the head of my dick on her wet pussy and tease her by just rubbing it in and out but not going all the way inside her. Just the head a little bit, and then rubbing it around the pussy.

"It's so wet" I tell her. She says to me "Put it in Good, stop teasing me".

I tell her "o.k. Sexy".

I slap her on the ass again and she jumps a little bit. Then I put it in all the way and she moans and groans.

First I start slowly. All the way in and then pull it almost all the way out. All the way in and then almost all the way out. Now it's put her ass to sleep time. I have already got a first nut so I can go for a little while longer this time.

I squeeze her waist and slap her on the ass several times as she makes the sounds of pleasure and I knew she was enjoying it. I caress her ass, thighs, calves, and feet. I see that it's driving her crazy and start with the poundy, poundy.

I grab her shoulder and then grab her hair to pull her head back. Now it's mercy hump time. Hump, hump, Bang. Hump, hump Bang. On every Bang she screams "Oh, yhea , yhea, Oh, yhea, yhea, Oh".

Now I go for the kill.

Bang. Bang. Bang. Bang. While she screams, "Oh, Oh, Oh, Oh".

I slap her on the ass and she screams "Oh, I'm going to cum". I slap her again on the ass while I pound the pussy and she screams "I'm Cuming' I'm Cuming".

"Yes, yes, yes, yes".

"Ooooohhhh, ooooohhhh, ooooooohhhh", she cums, as I can feel her pussy tightening and throbbing. But I'm not done yet. I tell her "I got you now". She says "no, no, no". I pound the pussy like a mad man and she loves it.

"Baby, baby ooooohhhh", she comes again. She tells me "You drive me crazy, You're driving me crazy". "Ooooooohhh, oooooooh".

I start to really bang the pussy. Like a wild animal on the Serengeti.

"Oh, yhea baby". I say. "Oh yhea baby", while slapping her on the ass. She's screaming and I'm moaning. I'm making all the yes sounds and she's going crazy.

I think that I was going to cum in a few so I place my thumb right on her ass hole. Not trying to put it inside but just to touch the outer hole.

She was going crazy. "Oh baby, oh baby". And starts to cum again I think.

I tell her that I'm going to cum. "I'm going to cum". She says "Cum daddy, cum on daddy".

She starts to feel the thickness of me inside her as it gets extremely hard before I cum. It's expanding and getting harder and harder and bigger and bigger.

She's screaming "Mercy, oh, Good, Good, oh, baby, baby. Oooohhhh, ooooohhh, Daddy".

I'm screaming "Yhea baby, yhea baby. Oooohhhh, yhea baby. You like that, you like that".

"I'm coming..... I'm coming"......

"Oooohhhhh", I scream "ooooooooh", she screams

I pound the pussy for a few more mercy humps as she jerks and screams on every hump.

I pull out and she lies down on the bed as I stand over her as if I had killed the pussy and wore her out.

I just stand there for a minute to catch my breath as she lays there trying to catch hers. I look at the clock and it's after midnight. I go into the bathroom to clean up a little and when I come out she is sound asleep. Another point for Mr. Goodnight.

I look at her and climb into bed with her. Scoot over real close to her so we could spoon. Put my arm around her and kiss her on the forehead. "Goodnight", I tell her and close my eyes too.

Chapter Three

When I wake up the next morning, she is already up and cooking something in the kitchen. I could smell coffee brewing and I think it was also some bacon cooking.

I get up to take a piss and wash my hands. Brush my teeth and use some mouth wash. I start for the kitchen and see that my pants were not where I put them last. I automatically think she has been in my pants. I grab them and go to the kitchen.

"Sexy", I called out. She answers back, "Hey baby I cooked for you". At that moment, I forgot all about what ever she went into my pants for. I looked at her standing there in one of my t-shirts with her long legs coming out from the bottom of the shirt and said to her. "Do you ever not look sexy"? She laughs and says "you're so crazy".

I move closer to her to see what she has cooking and she leans over to me and gives me a big kiss. I kiss her back and almost instantly get a hard on. What is it that is coming over me? I'm standing there in the kitchen and she's looking at me with my underwear on with a morning boner. She looks at me and says "come here and let me take care of that for you. Or do you want to eat first"? I can't make up my mind. Do I want to eat or do I want to fuck?

I am speechless. I could not say anything. She looks at me and comes over to me, grabs my hand and leads me to the table. Pulls out the chair and says sit here. I sit down in the chair and she goes back into the kitchen to finish cooking. All I could do was sit there and grin.

A moment later she comes out with two plates. Sets one in front of me and the other on the table were she was going to sit. I look at the plate and it smells so good. I have some grits, bacon, eggs and toast. This girl is a real lady and she can cook. I know that I didn't have any grits so I ask her as she sits down. "Were did you get the grits from"? She says back to me, "I took the keys out of your pocket and walked down to the corner market. I hope you didn't mind".

I looked at her with relief and say, "No, not at all baby". So we both start enjoying our morning breakfast and I tell her that she is a great cook and how this is very nice of her. She says back to me it was nothing. "I like to do things for my man". I start wondering if she just said that or does she think that I am her man now? I get up and go for something to drink. I see some orange juice that I know I didn't have. I say to her, "You bought some juice I see". She jumps up and says "Oh, that's right let me get it for you. Sit down and enjoy your breakfast".

I start for the table and wonder, could I get use to this. But I know that it always starts out like this and then it goes left and all hell breaks loose. So I finish my meal and she finishes hers too. All the while we just have small talk about music and traveling around the country. So I get up to clear my table and she jumps up and says "Oh, let me get that". She walks to the sink and puts both plates in. I place my cup on the counter and then gently hold her hand and make her look at me.

"Sexy, what are you trying to do here". She says "Nothing at all baby. I just like being nice, that's all". I look deeper into her eyes and say "Are you sure baby". She says, "Yes, I'm sure daddy", and touches me on the ass. "So I have to get ready for work, where would you like me to take you. Can I drop you off somewhere"?

She looks at me and says "Can you call off work today"? I touch her on the ass with both hands and say, "Is that right? You want me to call off work today"? She says, "Please daddy. I would like to spend some more time with you".

Looking at her very sexy body and temping lips. I tell her I can't do that. She says, "Why not"? And before you know it she has my dick in her hand and it is hard as wood. She says, "He doesn't want to go", pulling on my penis. I tell her that feels good. I then put both hands under the tee shirt and grab her ass while pulling her close to me.

I kiss her and she kisses me back. We both go down to the floor right there in the kitchen. She says in a tender voice. "Take me baby, right here, right now". I climb on top of her in the heat of passion from the kissing anticipating the wetness of her pussy. But wait, I didn't have any protection so I had to tell her wait a minute baby. "I'll be right back". She says you better hurry up.

I run into the bedroom and grab a rubber from the drawer and rush back into the kitchen. There she is on the floor waiting for me. She looked so sexy on the floor and I couldn't believe it so I tell her "Don't move I want to get a picture of you baby". I rush back into the room and grab my cell phone. Get back into the kitchen and point the camera at her. "Don't move baby", I take the picture.

I tell her to pull up the shirt just a little bit. She pulls up the shirt and I take another picture. She loves it. She pulls up the shirt all the way to expose that pretty pussy and I say "You sure have a beautiful pussy. Can I take a picture of it too"? She says "Yes, but you better not show no one".

I take a couple of pictures of her beautiful pussy and say now its time for some appreciation. I climb down to the floor and tell her to open wide. I am still hard and I open the rubber and slide it on. She says, "I don't like those things. They don't feel right". I say back to her, "I know. I don't like them either".

I ease inside of her and it feels so warm. She lays back and starts to make the humming sounds. "Mmmmmmm, that feels good daddy". I tell her the same. "Ooh yhea, you feel good to baby. Ooooohhhh, baby, it's so warm and wet". The slow motion of me in and out of her as she grinds back at me is starting to give me a floor burn.

So I hurry up the pace and pull her legs up over my head. She tells me to slow down, not so fast. I tell her that I have to go to work so I'm gonna make it quick. I lock her legs above my head and start pounding her tight little pussy. She is going wild and making the yes sounds again in a high pitch voice. It is turning me on so much that I know that I'm going to cum. "Oh, Oh, Oh, Oh". I start to pound and what do you know I could not hold it.

I cum and she loves it. She tells me, "Cum on daddy, cum on daddy. Yes, that's it, that's right. Cum inside me daddy". She is going to be trouble if I keep this up. I jump up and head for the bathroom. I jump into the shower and start signing. "A Million ways to please a woman."

After my shower, I start putting on my clothes and tell Sexy to get ready I have to leave soon. She starts getting ready and goes into the bathroom. So I'm ready and I'm waiting on her. I make fun and tell her "So this is what I look forward to in my life. Waiting for a woman. Always waiting for a woman". I laugh out loud. She says I'm ready, I'm ready let's go.

So we start for the car and I ask her "So where am I taking you baby". She tells me "I live right by Keys place". I answer "Is that right". She says "Yes, I live in the same building on the first floor". "Oh, o.k. Can I call you later tonight"? She says, "You better call me".

I pull up to her place and get out to open her door. I open the door to let her out and as she gets out she reaches out grabs me and gives me a great big hug and kiss. "Thanks for everything" I tell her. She answers, "Thank you Good, for everything. I had a really great time."

"I'll call you late Toots". I watch her head to the front door of the building and she gives me a switch that I know is for me. That ass jiggle's from left to right. Damn, that girl is fine. I get back into the car and head for work.

At work was a regular day, nothing special. Just work. So at lunch I decided to call Sexy up. "Hey Sexy, how are you"? She answers, "I'm good. How are you"? "I'm good too". She asks me if I could come by after work and I say "Sure. But this is what I want you to do when I come over". She says "What, anything Good. Just tell me what you would like".

I would love to come by after work. Have you open up the door for me with nothing on and greet me with a warm wet kiss. Pull me by my belt, into your bedroom, as I take off my shirt and tie on the way. As you close the door after I enter the bed room I grab you and force myself against you kissing your tender wanting lips. Focusing on your bottom lip, because it tastes so wet and sweet, you begin to unfasten my belt and drop my pants. I softly grab one of the twins and begin to lick it. Slow and gently at first, and then sucking harder and faster. I change one of the twins for the other and gently touch you down there to notice that it is very wet. I push you on the bed and look you in your eyes as I remove my underwear and stand there naked like you are my prey. I bend over slowly and kiss your lips. Then your neck, then your breast again. Then moving downward to your stomach, I start to tickle your navel with my tongue.

Spreading your legs apart I start to go down. Gently pressing my lips around your vagina. Kissing around it pulling at the fleshy lips.

There, I find your clit, sucking and licking it slowly. It taste very sweet and I want you more and more with every lick. Sucking and licking back and forth, faster and harder.

Now I am so hard and excited I have to have you. I climb on top of you looking into your sexy eyes as I start to grind your wetness. Gently finding your tight entrance I begin to enter inside you. Just the head at first, to know just how tight it really is.

Felling your wetness and warmth on my penis. Holding you as I now begin to penetrate slowly. Deeper, deeper in and out of you. Squeezing you harder and touching your every spot that I can feel. I change speeds slow and then fast. Listening for your sighs and moans I feel the heat of passion between me and you. You sigh and moan. I moan with you. Together we continue, more, more, yes, yes, yes, until we explode in pain of a orgasm together. We will cum together and then lay next to each other in ecstasy.

"Wow, Good. While you where telling me all that I had to touch myself and I almost came. You're a very bad man Good. So I will be waiting when you get off and I want that to happen just like that. O.k. I have to go baby. I will see you later tonight.

"Bye bye baby". She says.

"Later babe". I tell her and hang up the phone.

Oh, one more call to make. I have to call Baby. I dial the number and it rings a few times. She answers and I great her. "Hello Darling, how var you?" In the foreign voice.

She giggles and answers, "Hey Good how are you"? Sounding excited to hear from me.

"I'm good baby, I was just thinking about you". She says "Oh, really". "Yes, I can't stop thinking about you".

She answers, "is that right." I tell her, "I keep thinking about the rubber issue and how good it felt". She says "I know, I really enjoyed myself too Good".

I tell her "Hey listen, I had a dream that you came to me as I slept and kiss me. Your ever so gentle kiss woke me as I slowly started to reach out to you. With my eyes still shut I touch the softness of your beautiful skin and grab hold of you as my eyes begin to open, I see that it is you Baby. Those eyes and those lips. That pretty smile and I begin to pull you closer to me.

Wanting to feel you close to me, wanting more of those lips that had awaken me, I reach out with both hands now and begin to pull even harder and closer. I grab you and have you near me feeling that warm body of your against my naked body. I kiss those lips ever so gently looking into those eyes of yours and caress you slowly. I focus on your bottom lip, sucking it as I kiss both lips in the heat of a passion fire. Just as I squeeze you with a wanting you hug, I hear your soft sexy voice tell me yes. "Yes Good. Take me".

Then all of the sudden I woke up and you weren't there. I realized I was dreaming baby. You are really something special. I just want you to know that. Do you know that you're special"?

She answers, "Yes baby, if you say so". "Yes", I answer back. "I really think that you're special. You know I can't live my life without you. I really think I want to be your man". She stops me and says "wait a minute Good. Are you serious? Don't play with me."

I think about what I said and tell her "you know I may be a little sprung right now, I may need to think about this". She laughs at me. "You crazy Good", she says.

"Can I call you later Baby". She answers,

"Yes baby you can call me. I'll talk to you later. Bye bye Baby".

"Bye bye Good". I hang up the phone. Looking at the clock its time for me to go back to work. I walk back inside and finish work.

After work, I head for rehearsal. When I get there, I see Keys car parked in front. Keys is already there. I grab my sax and go inside. As I enter Keys says "There he is. What's up Good"? I grin at him and say back to him, "What's up!"

"Tell us about last night. I know you hit it. Where is she? Did you move her in"? All I could do is laugh because Keys knows me and I know him. After all, we are peter in-laws.

I start to set up and look at him and the other guys and say, "A gentleman never tells" in my foreign voice. We all laugh together very loud.

"Man", I say. "I got to say though. I really had to put in some work. Sexy is bad. And I owe it all to Keys. Keys were did you find that chick anyway"?

He laughs and says "Man she goes to my church". "Ooooohhhh". We all laugh together. "Man", I say. "A lady in the street and a freak in the bed".

"O.k. so let's kick off some tunes. One, two, three, four". And we all start playing together.

After rehearsal was over, I tell Keys and Keith "you guys gotta come to my place on Sun. so we can watch the game". We are all big L.A. Lakers Fans.

Everyone agrees and says o.k. "I'm there, me too. We need to bring anything"? "Naw man, I got yall. Just show up". I know what they like to drink and eat because we like the same things. We have a lot in common. We like the same kind of women, food, drink, and music.

When I get home that night, I call Lil Mama to see what she is doing. I haven't talked to her in a long time. Even though we have had sex several times she still is my confidant and I can talk to her about anything. Even other women.

"Hey Lil Mama, what's good wit cha"? She answers very excited. "Good, what's going on? Why you can't call a bitch"? I laugh. "I have been busy baby". She laughs and says "yhea, busy Fucking bitches". We laugh together. "When you gone come see a bitch. You know a bitch need her fix". I answer. "I'm gone come see you. I promise."

"So what's up"? She says.

"My homies gone be over on Sun to watch the game, you wanna come by"? "What you gone have fo a bitch to eat"? she says. "You gone cook some gumbo nigga"? I tell her "If you promise to come by I will cook you some gumbo for you baby."

She laughs and says "I'm there my nigga".

"So it's a rap. I'll see you on Sun".

"See you on Sunday Good". "See you on Sunday Lil Mama".

I hang up the phone and look in the mirror and tell myself. "They aint gonna be ready for this."

I go to the kitchen and fix me a sandwich. Pour me a glass of carrot juice and turn on the TV. Flip thru some channels and stop at a movie that's on. Not really into the movie, I finish my sandwich and drink down the carrot juice. I grab the phone because I can not get Baby off my mind. Is it because I put in so much work to get the pussy?

I think if I had not put in so much time and conversation before I got the pussy. I would not have her on my mind. Maybe the pussy was just that good? I mean I had some good pussy before but she got the bomb. Could I be really sprung? I mean she is beautiful. She is smart. She is educated and successful. Maybe this is really the one and I need to hang up my players' card. Maybe I'm getting out of touch and I need to get a grasp on life. Maybe I should think about getting married and having kids.

The movie I was watching started watching me as I had fallen asleep. I woke up later in the middle of the night with a hard on. Baby was on my mind. I grab the phone look at the time and it says two o'clock am.

I wanted to just hear her voice so I called her knowing that she probably wouldn't answer the phone. Her voice mail answers so I leave a message.

"Hey Baby, its good. I fell asleep and just woke up. Its 2 o'clock in the morning. I'll call you in the morning babe. Have a good one".

I call her right back to leave another message.

I want to tell her I was thinking about her and she gave me a hard on. Some time women like when you be a man and tell them really what's on your mind.

So the phone rings and she answers this time.

"Hello", sounding very sleep.

"Hey Baby, I just wanted to hear your voice".

She tells me to call her tomorrow and that she is sleep.

I tell her "Goodnight baby, Goodnight".

I hang up the phone and get up and stretch.

I get in the bed and fall asleep thinking of Baby.

Chapter Four

My alarm goes off in the morning and I start getting ready for work. As I walk out the door headed for work I remember I have to call Baby.

So I call her on the way to work on my blue tooth. The phone rings and she answers.

"Hello" she says.

"Hello Darling", in my foreign voice. She laughs.

"Hey Good, how are you"?

"I'm fine now thank you". She laughs again.

"You are so crazy Good".

"Crazy about you Baby". I start singing

"Crazy, bout yo Love". She laughs some more.

"Hey", She says "what"?

"I was thinking about you all night. When I called you and you answered the phone sleep, I wanted to crawl inside your bed naked. Scoot closer to you and press my body against your naked body. Kissing your face at first and then your neck, then your shoulder, then your breast. Oh, the taste of your nipple is such an aphrodisiac I grind myself against you.

Rubbing me against you makes it even so harder that I have to have you. I go down kissing your navel and spreading your legs. You touch me as if you want it. I hear you call my name. "Ooooh Good".

"Yes Baby", I answer as I start to kiss your flesh slowly and gently, separating your lips apart with my tongue as if searching for that spot.

There it is and it taste so good. Warm, wet and tasty. I make you squirm and you start to grind me. Moving back and forth as if you can't stand it anymore, you tell me you want me inside you. "Put it inside me" you beg me for it.

I start upward to kiss the twins and you grab for my penis to put it inside you. It is so hard and it feels so good when you touch it. You kiss me as you put me inside you. Oh, it feels so warm and tight. I begin to penetrate and you grind me back. Both of us humping each other in the moment, It hot and steamy love making time.

I kiss you and you kiss me back moaning and groaning. We both start to rise to a climax together. Yes, it's Cuming. It's Cuming, its Cuming. We both shake and quiver and explode together at the same time. I squeeze you and you squeeze me back harder. Oh, I can't take it and you won't let me go as you start to grind some more. Slowly I kiss you and grind back slowly with you. Love has its way into our hearts and body.

"Damn, Good. I love it when you talk like that.
My pussy is so wet now".

"Damn, I want to fuck. Can you come to my job for lunch"? "Yhea Baby. I'm there. You sure you want to do this"? She laughs and says "Yhea. Call me before you come".

"Ok, I'll call you later Baby".

"Bye Good, you have a good day, I will see you later daddy".

"Bye Baby".

I hang up the phone with the biggest grin on my face.

So I get to work and there is a police car in the parking lot. This is different. I try to see what's going on. There are some people talking to the officer. I see one of my co-workers Dan. "Hey Dan, what's happening". He laughs and says. "Man, you missed it. Two chicks were out here boxing it out. Pulling hair, kicking, slapping, punching and scratching".

"Man, do you know who they were"? I asked.

"No, man. I never seen them before. Just some loud ass black chicks".

Wow, I wonder what the hell was going on.

I go inside to clock in and I see my good buddy Chris. "Hey Chris", I say to him.

"Good, man you aint gonna believe this shit". He says.

"You know that girl that you had introduced me to last month".

"You mean Crissy". "Yhea, that's that bitch. Crissy". He replies.

"What's up with Crissy"? I say.

"Man, that bitch came up her and started some shit with my girl". "What"! I answer in disbelief. "I told you that bitch was crazy".

"Man, I should have listened to you Good. Are the police still out there"?
"Yhea man, they are still out there. Did anyone see anything"? I ask.

He replies, "No man. It was just me, my girl and then that bitch pulls up and takes out a bat. Started swinging it around at my girl. So I grab the bat and my girl starts kicking her ass, Saying bitch I told you to stay away from my man. I had to break it up but man; I had to let my girl get in some good ones though". He laughs and smiles.

"Man, she got some bomb head though".

"I know what you mean Chris. But I had to cut her short. I could see the signs that bitch was crazy".

"Yhea", he answers, "I saw them too. When that bitch pulled a knife out on me, I should have been done with her then. But I had to keep on playin with fire.
Man, Good. Why you never get caught up"?

I look at him and said. "A player never gets played". "You can't play a player".
He looks at me and says "Fo Sho Player".
We slap hands and go our way. "Peace Chris".

"Peace Good".

Later it's about lunch time and I tell me boss I will be late from lunch maybe, I have to go across town. She tells me o.k. But then says "You're gonna owe me one".

I agree, "anytime".

So I call Baby up on the phone. The phone rings. She answers.

"Hello".

"Hello Darling", I answer in my foreign voice.

"Good, how are you"? She replies.

"I'm bedy good, yes". I reply in my foreign voice.

She laughs.

"So you comin to see me right". She asks.

"Yes darling". I answer. "How do I get there"?

She gives me directions and I tell her that I'm on my way I will call her when I get there.

She says "O.k. I will see you soon baby".

"O.k., later Baby". We hang up the phones.

I leave and get into my whip and head for downtown. When I get there I call Baby. She answers the phone and I tell her I'm in the parking lot. She says come inside and go up to the 6th floor. Room 616. I'm in my office.

I enter the building and head for the elevators. The lobby guard stops me and says you have to sign in please. I sign in and head for the elevator. Everyone is leaving for lunch. I am the only one going into the building.

The door opens and I press the number six. The elevator starts to go up and I watch the numbers on the top of the door. Ding, ding, ding, I get to the 6th floor and the elevator stops and the doors open.

I exit the elevator and look for the door 616. I find it and knock on the door. No one answers so I turn the knob and walk in. There is a front desk in the front room. The room behind the desk is where I see Baby sitting. She sees me and says "Come in Good".

I walk in and she's sitting at the desk signing some papers looking very executive like. With glasses on and her hair pulled back into a pony tail. I walk over to her desk and tell her I love a woman in a suit. And laugh.

She stops writing and looks at me and says go lock the door as she stands up. I turn around and walk to the door to lock it. She comes from around the table and I can see she has on a very short skirt to her suit. I walk towards her and she says "I've been thinking about your all day Good."

I look her in her eyes and say "Me too Baby".

We connect at the lips and start to kiss passionately. I am already excited and she knows it when she touches my pants. I back her up to her desk and say to her. "You want it here baby"?

She says "Yes take me, take me now. I'm not wearing any panties".

I pull up her skirt and to my surprise she is not wearing any panties. She unzips my pants and pulls out my erect penis. I unbuckle my pants and drop them to the floor with my underwear. I sit her on the edge of the desk as if I had mounted her. I was ready for the taking.

She has her arms around me by the neck and legs up around my waist. I open her blouse and start kissing her tities. She tells me to put it in. "Put it in Good". I touch her pussy and it is so wet and warm. I ease the head of me into her wet pussy and she gives me a sound of yes.

"Oooohhh, that feels so good Good". I enter a little farther into the warmth as she says "Yes baby", then I ease it out. In and out slowly we go as she is excited and stats to tell me. "Fuck me daddy, Fuck me". I start in and out a little faster and faster as she starts with the yes sounds. "Yes, yes daddy. Ooh, yes daddy".

She clinches around my neck tighter and her legs tighten up around me. She starts to tremble as I start to pound in the pussy. I know that she is either going to cum or she is already Cuming. She starts with the ooooohhhh, shit. I know for a fact that she is Cuming now, so I get with the poundy, poundy.

I pound the pussy like I'm trying to knock a hole out the other side. "Emph, emph, emph. Yhea baby, yhea baby. Emph, oh, yhea there, there, oh, I'm Cuming baby". I explode inside her and keep on humping the last few mercy humps.

"Oh, yhea, oh yhea" as I start to slow down. The pussy is so tight as I stop I tell her to let me go. She lets my neck go and has her hands on my shoulders now. Unlocks her legs and I tell her "Tell your pussy to let me go". We both start laughing so hard. I then slowly pull out my penis as she reaches for some tissue she has on her desk. She grabs a few and hands them to me.

"Thanks Baby". I accept the tissue and wipe off my dick. "Ooohh, that was great Baby". She looks at me and says "Did you like that". I look at her and say "I loved it".

"Was it good for you too baby"? She looks at me staring me in the eyes and says "I thought you knew daddy".

I tell her as I look at the clock, "I have to go Baby. I'll call you later Toots".

She says ok and thanks me. "Thank you Good, Talk to you later daddy".

As I'm leaving the building out the lobby area, I can't help but notice this very attractive woman wearing all red. She is walking in my direct path towards me. She has the most amazing body. She has a very small waist and a very cute face.

As I get closer to her I walk in front of her and say "Excuse me, I'm sorry but can I have your phone number? I'm just kidding, unless your gonna give it to me".

She smiles. I tell her "My name is Good. What's your name"? She tells me "My name is Denise". "I'm sorry Denise but you are extremely beautiful, can I call you later please. I have to really run. I mean I don't work here and I may never see you again". She says "Why are you here"?

I tell her, "Well I came here to see a friend and yes she is a woman. I don't want to sound like a dog but I was going to hate myself if I didn't at least ask you your name". "Well Mr. Good, I don't think so" she says. "I tell you what", I answer. "I don't see a ring on that finger so can I invite you to one of my performances". She starts to look interested and says "Are you a singer or something"?

"I am a sexologist, I mean saxologist". "I play the saxophone". She smiles and her smile is so beautiful.

"You have the most beautiful smile Denise". She starts to look for something to write with. I whip out a pen and a piece of paper. She says "That was fast".

I answer, "I don't have time to waste. I am a very busy man". She gives me her number and I tell her that I will call her later as I scurry out of the building. I get into the car thinking got another victim. Danm, she was fine. Denise, Denise.... I start the car and head back to work.

I finish my day at work and start for home. No rehearsal tonight so I'm just going to kick it at the pad. Oh, shit. I almost forgot I have to go by and see Sexy. So I reach my home and call Sexy up on the phone. Ring, ring, ring. "Hello" she answers.

"Hey Sexy, how var you darling"? In my foreign voice. She laughs and says "Good, Good" sounding very excited to hear my voice. "So are you coming by"? She says.

"Sure, what's your apartment number"? "It's 112" she answers. "O.k. I'll see you in a couple hours". "O.k. Good, I'll see you when you get here". I ask her if there's anything that she wants me to bring and she says "Just bring yourself". I tell her "You got it babe. See you later". She says "Bye" and hangs up the phone.

I get out my laptop and turn it on to check my emails. When I check my emails I have 14 new emails. I start to go threw them and notice that I have one from The Boom Boom Room. It's a really nice spot that has live music, drinks and they also serve food.

The email reads,

Dear Mr. Goodnight,

We are happy to inform you that we have accepted your invitation to perform at our establishment. Your video tells us that you have quite a showmanship with your band and we would love to have you do your thing for us.

Your price of $1500 per night is very reasonable per your status.

Please get in touch with our manager at the property for dates and times.

Again, thank you for your interest in our establishment.

See you soon.

District Manager

Mr. Powers

I was so excited to read this email; I had to call the fellas. Wait, I'll send out a copy of the email first to all the guys on the band. I forwarded the email to all the guys and then called them one by one.

"Keys, we got the gig at the Boom Boom Room. We gotta video it man. This is going to be the shit". Keys screams out loud, "Yhea baby" as if he scored a touchdown.

I call Left, the Bass player.

"Left, we got the gig at the Boom Boom Room". "Word", he answers. "How much they payin? I tell him "We gone get $300 each per night, Fri, Sat and Sun".
He starts singing "Money, money, money, MONEY". I tell him "I got to call Sticks" and hang up.

I call up Sticks and he answers. "Sticks, what's good man"? "Hey Good", her answers.

I tell him, "We got the gig at the Boom Boom Room man. He says "18 Karat".

I say "what"? He says, "You know, 18 Karat, as in full out, all the way, awesome".

I answer, "Oh, O.k.". And we laugh. Sticks is kinda out there in this jazz thing that we have a brotherhood in. He talks in a lot of slang or what they call Hip talk.

I call up Quick. He's our guitar player. "Hey Quick, its Good, what it do"?
He answers, "Yo Good what's happening"?
I tell him, "Man we got the Gig at the Boom Boom Room".
He yells out "SUPERMURGITROID".

I bust out laughing and he does also. I tell him "Don't snap yo cap".

He laughs and says you mean, don't blow your top. I say "It's the same thing and he argues, No its not. We both start laughing again.

He asks me, "How much is it paying"?
I tell him its paying the amount we talked about. $300 each night, Friday, Saturday and Sunday. That's $900 per weekend.

He says, " We gonna play more than one weekend"?

I tell him that it depends on how well things go off. If we blow the roof off the house, I'm sure that he will want us to come back. He was really impressed with our promo DVD.

He loves us. I sent you and the rest of the guys a forward of the email he sent me.

"Straight", he replies.

"Alright Man, I'll see you tomorrow at rehearsal".

"All right Good, see you tomorrow". He says before he hangs up the phone.

I sit back and think about the upcoming show. Thinking we have to video this show.

I think about Sexy and remember I am supposed to see her tonight. So I jump into the shower and get ready for Sexy. Out of the shower and into the closet. I pull out some sharp threads because I want to look good for her. I put on some smell good and brush my teeth and gargle with some mouth wash. "I'm ready" as I look into the mirror adjusting my final touches. I call up Sexy to see if she's ready to see me.

Ring, ring.

"Hello Darling, how var you"? In my foreign voice. She repeats me, "Hello Darling", trying to sound like me. I laugh out loud.

She says "Get over here Good. I know you aint gonna have a girl waiting".

I tell her "I'm on my way sexy Sexy".

Chapter Five

I head for my whip and jump inside and hit a corner or two. I get to Sexy's building and start for her apartment. I have to ring in because the place is gated. I ring her and she buzzes me in. as I enter the building I see an old friend. It's Tonya.

"Hey Tonya, how are you"? She replies "Good, how are you? It's been so long".
"I've been good. You know that s my name, I'm always good". And laugh out loud.

She says you have to call me sometime. So I ask her for her number and she says "come, let's go inside and I'll write it down". So I follow her into her apartment and as we enter there is a beautiful lady sitting at the table.

I suddenly say, "Look what the cat drug in".
The beautiful lady at the table says, "Is there any more outside like him? Can you drag one in for me too"?

I smile and Tonya says "Good, I want you to meet my sister Tangy. Tangy. This is Good".

I look into her eyes and say, "Nice to meet you".

So Tonya writes the number down and I say I will call you later and leave because I didn't want to keep Sexy waiting. I get to Sexy's door and knock and she answers the door and greats me with open arms. Gives me a great big hug and pulls me in. She looks at me and says "I've been thinking about you all day Good". I tell her "Me too".

She says, "mmmmm you smell good. What do you have on"? As she rubs on my face and chest, I tell her, "I have on some smell good called Clive Christian. It cost $2,350.00

Her eyes get really big and she says you got to be kidding me.

I tell her "No I'm serious".
She says "You paid $2,350 dollars for some cologne? I tell her "No baby, it was a gift from a good friend".

She says "I bet it was some woman". I laugh and say "are you jealous"?

She gives me an unbelievable look and says "no, I'm not jealous" while she shakes her head. I can plainly see that she is jealous but I pay it no never mind.

I walk toward her and look at her in the eyes. I tell her that nobody is sexier than you. You are the definition of sexy. She looks at me and smiles. I go on to say when I'm near you; you take me on a Sexual high. She holds my hands now and starts to light up. "Good", she says. "You really now how to make me smile. You make love to my mind, my body and my soul. You are really something special".

She starts to lead me into her bedroom and ask me if I was thirsty or hungry. I tell her that all I need is her to satisfy me. I can live on her alone. She says "Good you are so full of shit, but I like it".

She turns off the light and turns on the TV. Puts in a DVD of some adult porn. She says "I hope that you don't mind but I would like to give you a special treat tonight".

I answer, "I don't mind at all baby. You do your thing. But I thought women didn't like porn". She looks at me and says "I don't really watch it but this girl did some really different stuff and I wanted to try it on you. Porn is nasty, just a bunch of sluts and ho's who can't find anything better to do".

She comes over and stands in front of me and says "do you think I'm sexy"?

I answer "I sure do baby. Come here and let me show you."

I place my hands inside her shirt and pull the shirt out of her pants. She says wait. "I want to change into something more comfortable". She goes into a drawer and pulls out some lingerie. Goes into the bathroom to change and comes back out with a very seductive black teddy.

As she gets closer she says "now, do you think I'm sexy?"

I just stare at her before I speak and say "Damn Sexy, you are super sexy" with my mouth open. She turns around and says "Do you like? I reply, "Yes darling", in my foreign voice. I stand up and start to walk towards her and she says "Stop right there. Take off your shirt" she tells me. I stop in my tracks and take off my shirt.

Before I could take it off all the way she says also take off your shoes. So I take my shoes off also. There she is undressing me with her words. Off with my t-shirt. There goes my pants, as she turns around touching herself. In the background I suddenly notice the music on the TV. It's smooth and silky sounding.

I'm standing there in my underwear. She ask me in a smooth sexy voice "So, do you want this body"? I start moving to her as she starts to back up. I corner her back against the wall and inch my lips close to hers. I whisper softly in her ear. "Nobody can love you like I do".

I kiss her and she kisses me back. We slowly join tongues and begin our slow erotic climax to ecstasy together. I know that she will please me as I will surely please her. We are very compatible when it comes to pleasing each other. She gives me her mmmmmm sound and I respond with a hum like hers.

We start moving to the bed as my hands are all over her. She's grabbing me all over and I'm grabbing her too. We reach the bed and I throw her to the bed and she screams "Oh". I lean over her to kiss her and she puts her hands around my neck and pulls my arms toward her.

Her hands are now on my ass as she squeezes my butt cheeks. I kiss her on her neck and she sounds off like a fire alarm. "Yes, Good. Take me, I am yours". I lick her nipples that are all ready showing because her teddy is cut out at the breast area. She loves it as her nipples are hard like pencil erasers. I gently bite the tips of her nipples as she tells me "Yes daddy. That feels good". I tell her to scoot up on the bed. "Scoot up some more baby".

I stand up and pull off my underwear as she looks at me from the bed. She says, "Come and get it daddy" as she opens her legs to show me that she has on a crotch less opening on her teddy.

The pussy is so pretty. Her hair is so neatly cut and trimmed. At that moment I want to kiss and suck her pretty pussy. I get closer to her and grab one of her long legs. I start on the top of her foot. I kiss it. Then I lick it to the tip of her big toe. I place the big toe into my mouth sucking on it. She moves as if she can't take it but I will not let go or stop. I start on the next toe, kissing and sucking it. Then the next one and the next one as she moans and groans moving around like a fish out of water.

Her hands are clinched to the covers so tightly. I start to kiss up her leg and she says "Oh, Good. You make me so wet. You're driving me crazy".

I get to her knee and start licking it in a circular motion, kissing it on the inner side. I move up the inner side of her leg slowly kissing every inch of her leg till I get close to the vagina.

Now I have both her thighs on each side of my face, so I lick the inner thighs and kiss them. I lock on the left thigh sucking it as if I am going to give her a monkey bite. I let go and I can see that she bruises easily.

I start for the vagina. I lick around the fleshy parts as if I'm looking for something. "Where is that clit" I ask her? "Mmmm, where is it"? I lick on the clit and say "Mmmmm, there it is", as she moans. "Oooohhh, yes, that's it".

I lick up and down slowly. Making sure not to go inside just yet. She tells me "You're driving me crazy Good". Her pussy is on fire and she is very wet now. I lock in on her clit and lick it gently at first. Then I lick it a little more firmly. Then I begin to suck it as she starts to moan and groan louder. "Oohh, Good. That feels so good baby".

I start the quick tickler on the clit and she grabs my ears. "Yes daddy, that's it. Yes daddy". I lick soft then hard, softer and then harder. Sucking and licking at the same time.

Then I give her an unexpected lick into the pussy hole really quick and back to the clit. She explodes in ecstasy as she lets me go and grabs the covers on her bed. She screams "I'm Cuming, I'm Cuming". I grab hold of her ass as if I have a lock on her. She tries to push me away from her but I have a firm lock on that ass. She cums more and more. And I start to slow down to a lick like she was a Popsicle.

Slower and slower, I start licking up and down. She moans and groans "Oh, daddy. Mmmmm that's was so good. Oh, Good you are so good to me."

She then jumps up and pushes me over on my back and climbs on top of me kissing me in the mouth. She says "I got a treat for you too". She kisses me on the neck and then my chest. Licking my nipples and then down to my stomach. She pulls of my underwear and grabs my dick gently as she puts it in her mouth. Pulls it out and says "Ooh you taste so good".

She licks my penis up to the tip and down to my balls. Then she starts on my nut sack, sucking one and then the other nut. I tell her "That's right baby, that feels good."

She says "Wait a second". Gets up and opens a drawer and pulls out a small glass with a bottle of Tanqueray Gin in it.

She brings it over to me and says "I want to please you Good". She starts sucking me again and tells me "Please don't cum in my mouth. Tell me when you going to cum ok". I say "ok". And she says "You promise" as she's sucking on my dick and I say "Yhea baby I promise".

As she's sucking my dick it feels so good as she's changing directions. Up and down, softer and harder. In and out of her mouth. She starts to even stroke me at the same time she sucks it. "Damn Sexy, that feels so good. You're gonna make me cum". She says "That's it baby. Cum for me daddy. But not in my mouth. Let me know when you're almost Cuming".

I moan and groan as she hums with me inside her mouth. She loves it as much as I do. My elevation is reaching its peak as all the blood in my penis is now reaching the head and its hard as steel. I inform her that I am almost Cuming. She says "Cum on daddy".

"Almost baby, almost baby". She grabs the glass and that's when I tell her "Ok baby, I'm there". She pulls my dick out of her mouth and puts the glass under the head. She jacks me off as I bust a big fat nut. She is putting my entire nut in the glass as if she was milking a cow or something. She was milking me.

"That's right daddy" she says. "Give me every bit of it", as I moan and grown. "Oooohhh, baby. Yes, Sexy". She says "Is that it? I think that's all your cum".

I am leaning up on my elbows now looking at what the hell she is doing, and I see the glass with my cum in it.

Then she grabs the Tanqueray and opens it. Pours some of it into the glass with my sperm. Sticks her finger in the glass and swishes it around a few times. Licks her finger, and drinks the glass of Gin and sperm.

Down the hatch in one gulp like it was her favorite drink. "Damn…. Damn Sexy", I say in unbelief.

She wipes her lips and says "That was good". She says "Now that's what I call Good-Gin".

I lie back on the bed and start cracking up. She jumps on top of me and says give me kiss. I can't push her away because I am hysterical. She climbs on me and starts kissing me on the neck and we start wresting around the bed. I tell her "I got to tell me boys about this". She says you better not. You better not tell anyone. I push her away from me and say "Man; I still don't believe that just happened".

We lay there together gently touching each other, caressing and rubbing one another. I tell her "You know I am really hungry now. Do you have anything to eat"?

She says "I could make you a sandwich with some turkey". I tell her "Cool, I love turkey". As she gets up to go into the kitchen, I give her a slap on the ass and watch it jiggle. I tell her as she walks out of the room "I love your juicy ass. You really have a nice ass baby".

As I lay there in awe of what had just happened, I think about the show. When she walks into the room after making the sandwich I tell her. "You know you have a really nice ass". She says "If you say so Good". I ask her, "You gone give me some ass one day"? She looks at me and says "I'm gonna have to drink a lot of gin for that to happen."

So I take that as yhea boy, you gone get that ass one day? She didn't say no.

Men love a woman's ass. It's not a homosexual thing; it's a tight, jiggley, very personal thing between me and my sexual partner. Anal sex is a different, tighter sensation. Women either love it or hate it. She moans, screams and groans, acting like your killing her. But pain can be very good sometimes. Have you ever heard the expression "it hurts so good".

I tell her "Bye the way, we have gig coming up at the Boom Boom room". She lights up with delight. "Oh, really". "Yhea, I found out today". She says "Maybe I can sign with you guys". I tell her "Some things you never know". And she just smiles ear to ear.

She comes over to me and says "You need some more attention". I tell her "Let me eat my sandwich first". She says o.k. and asks me if I want something to drink. "What do you have" I answer. She says "I have some water and some ruby red". I tell her "I would love some ruby red".

She goes into the kitchen and brings back the ruby red and hands it to me. I take a drink and put the sandwich down. Look her in her eyes and tell her, "Sexy, you are really something special". As I kiss her on the lips. She hugs me and we turn over for round two.

I hold the twins and start to kiss and lick them. They are so soft and taste so sweet and firm to the tip. I am instantly hard again. I turn her over and rub my dick into her vagina. Just the head at first then inch it in one inch at a time. The pussy is so wet and tight. We both moan, "Oooohh, yes". "Oh, baby". "Yhea baby".

Humping and grinding on each other the temperature heats up. She lifts her knees higher as I pump and hump faster and harder. She loves it when I beat up the pussy. Slow at first but very ruff at the end.

I now have her ankles up above my head, spread apart and I'm pounding the pussy.

"Ummph, umph, ooohh, yhea baby".

"Get it daddy" she says. "That's your pussy, get it daddy".

"Yes, baby. Oh, it's so good Good".

I grab her toes with on of my hands and pull them back. She makes an oohh, yes sound.

As I let go off her toes she screams, "Oh, yes. I'm Cumming, I'm Cumming"? "Oooowwww, oooohhh, yeeeesssss".

Her legs start to tremble as if she is going into convulsions as I hold her legs up in the air, still humping and pounding inside of her.

Then all this good sounding sex really turned me on, so I can't help but to climax only moments later. "Oh, yhea baby. I'm Cumming too. Ooww. Yes. Yes. Oooohhhh". I cum and push my dick all the way inside of her and she screams too with me. Together in almost harmony we scream in ecstasy. "Yes".

We are locked together and can't move. Then I try to move by pulling out and she says "Don't move baby" while holding me close. I pull out slowly and she lets go. I get up and move the bathroom where I clean up myself. After I finish cleaning myself up, I put back on my clothes and tell her that I have to get home. She says that she doesn't want me to leave. I tell her that I have to go but I will call her later. She says bye and I leave out the door. I exit the building and open my car door. Get inside my car and start up the engine. Put the car in drive and head for the pad.

When I get home I call up Tonya, the girl that I had met earlier that night. Ring, ring, "Hello". A sexy voice answers.

"Hello darling, in my foreign voice. "Hello", she answers again.

"May I speak to Tonya"? I say.

"Tonya's not here". She tells me.

"Could you tell that Good called please". I ask her.

"Ok", she says.

"Is this Tangy"? I ask.

"Yes", she answers.

"How are you"? I ask her.

"I'm fine, thank you". She replies.

"This is Good, the guy that you met earlier".

"Oh, hi Good". "I will tell her that you called".

"Ok, bye". Then I hang up the phone and lay it down.

I reminisce about the day until I fall asleep.

Chapter Six

The next day is Saturday and I get up and look out the window. It is a beautiful day outside. The sun is shining and it looks like it is very warm.

I start getting ready for a great Saturday. First things first, I call up my boys and see what's poppin today.

I call Keys first.

"Keys, what's good man"? "Hey Good, what it do"?

"What's crackin today"? "Man, I'm gone to a jam session tonight. You want to go; it's gone be the shit".

"Maybe, where is it gonna be"? "It's gonna be at Sticks place". "Oh, ok. Maybe I'll see you there man". "Alright, later man. Peace out".

I then call Sticks. "Sticks, what happenin"?

"I may come thru tonight for your jam session". "Straight dude", he answers. "I'll see you later then man". "Good". "Alright then, I'll see you later man".

"Later". We hang up the phones.

I then call Left the bass player. Ring, ring,

"Hello" he answers. I say, "Hey Left, what's up man"? "Good"? He asks. "What's good wit you man"?

I answer, "I just called to see what's up with you man". "Not much man" he says. "I might go to the beach and get some sunshine and panty lines".

I answer, "Now that's what I'm talking bout man. What time you goin"? I ask.

"Oh, about noon man, are you commin"? I answer, "Yhea man, I'll see you later man. Cool"? He replies, "Cool".

"Alright, later". He answers, "Later Good". We hang up and I call up the guitar player Quick.

Ring, ring, "Yo", he answers.

"Quick, what's good? It's Good". He answers. "Hey man, what it do"? I tell him that I and Left are going to the beach around noon. He says "Man, I wish I could go. I have to take my girl to the mall to do some shopping". I answer, "Alright man, I understand. You got to do what you got to do. I'll call you up later man". He says.

"Alright then, later man".

"Later", I say and hang up the phone.

So I start to fix me something to eat and get my day rolling. I go to turn on some music and dial up some Boney James. So I smother me some potatoes with onions and put some sliced smoked sausage in it. While I'm letting the potatoes smother. I call up Lil Mama.

Ring, ring, ring. "Hello" she answers the phone.

"Hey Lil Mama, what's happenin"? She replies, "Oh, nothing man. Just chillin". I ask her if she is still coming over tomorrow. And she says "Are you still cookin me some gumbo"? "Yhea baby, I'm gone still cook your gumbo". She says "Well then I'm there".

She ask me if my boys are gone be there too still? And I tell her that they are gone be there, cause we gonna be watching the game. She says "Alright baby, I'll see you tomorrow morning around 10 o'clock". I answer; "I'll see yo ass tomorrow then babe". She says bye and I tell her bye and we both hang up our phones.

I finish cooking my potatoes and fix my plate. Sat at the table and got out the hot sauce and ketchup. I start to eat and the phone rings. It's Baby.

"Hello Darling. How var you"?
She answers, "Hey Good, how are you"? I tell her "I'm fine but not as fine as you are".

"What you doing today beautiful"? I ask her. She says "I going to the mall and then I have to go see my Mom". I say "When can I see yo pretty self"? She answers "Maybe later tonight".

I tell her that I was going to go to a jam session and she says "Wow, I never been to a jam session." And then she asks if she can go. I tell her "Sure you can", without thinking.

"I'll call you later babe". She says bye and we both hang up our phones.

As I'm eating the rest of my potatoes I suddenly think what's going to happen if Keys brings Sexy. So I call Keys and ask him if he's going to bring anyone to the jam session and he says no. Cool, I don't have anything to worry about. So I tell him that I will see him later. I finish my plate and leave to go get some ingredients for the gumbo.

When I get to the store I grab a basket and head for the meat section. I get some shrimp, crab, andouille sausage and some boneless chicken. I go to the produce section and get some onions, celery, green bell peppers and some gumbo file. I think about if I am missing anything and then head for the register.

When I get to the register there is a very cute young lady ringing up everyone. She starts ringing up my stuff and says "Hello, how are you"?

I reply "I'm good". She says "Someone's makin Gumbo huh"? I tell her "Yes I am making gumbo, how did you know"? She looks with a surprised face and says "You can cook"? I tell her "Yes, I can cook". She gives me the biggest smile. I tell her "You can come by and get a taste if you want". She says "Don't try me because I'll come by and get me some".

I ask her for her pen and write my number on the receipt that she gives me and tell her "It's goin down tomorrow afternoon". She smiles and says what's your name?

I say "Good" and she smiles again and tell me "Alright Mr. Good" as she puts the number in her jeans pocket. As I bag my stuff up, I can see behind the counter and notice that she has a very nice ass. I could not stop looking at it. She turns around a catches me looking at her ass. I try to act like I was not looking and say "I'm sorry I could not help myself". And she smiles and tells me "That's o.k."

I'm trying to keep myself focused. And then I smile back at her and tell her "Make sure you call me. What's your name again"? She tells me her name is Alize'. I smile and walk away as she watches me.

I take the groceries back to my place and put them away. I call up Tonya again to see what's up with her.

Ring, ring, ring, "Hello". A sexy voice answers. "Hello, is Tonya there"? I ask.

"No, she isn't" the voice replies.

"Could you tell her that Good called" I ask her.

"Oh, hello Good, this is her sister Tangy again".

"Hey Tangy, how are you"? I ask her. She answers, "I'm great. How are you"?

"I'm always good baby", I answer in a joking way.

"Do you know when I can catch her home"?
She tells me "I don't know. But I will tell her that you called".

I ask her if she told Tonya that I called before, and she says "yhea, I did".

"Oh, o.k., I guess I'll talk to her later. So what are you doing"? I ask her.

"Nothing, just some school work I have to finish. I have finals coming up soon". She replies.

I ask her "What school do you go too"? And she tells me "I go to CSUN".

"Oh, I went to High School down the street for CSUN". I answer back. So I tell her that I will try to call back later and she says ok. We both say goodbye and I think did we just have a connection there?

Chapter Seven

I hit up Left and ask if he's ready for the beach. He tells me "Yhea" and I tell him that "I'll be right over to pick him up".

I get to his place and call him to come out. He tells me he will be right out. He comes out and gets in the car and we head to the beach.

We arrive at the beach and there is nowhere to park. I tell him I know a spot we can park by Gold's gym. He says "Yhea, I know that spot. I parked there before".

So we find a spot and park but we have to walk a few blocks to the beach. Down the street we walk, across the street and down an alley till we get there. We reach the beach.

"Man, its all kinds of people out here". I say.

He says man it pretty hot too. I agree as we walk down the walkway. Look, there is the dude that stands on glass he says.

Man, look at that chick with the see through scarf wrapped around her bikini. Man, look at these two babes coming right at us.

"Hey ladies, how are you"? I say. They just smile back at us and keep walking. Everybody knows that women are eye candy at the beach. Then all of the sudden I grab Left.

"Left, look man" I say.

"What" he replies?

"Them bitches got they tities showin.

"Where," he says. And I point to them.

"Danm, man. They got there nips covered though." "Man, she got some pretty tits." "Look man, there go some more."

And we start noticing as we walk closer to the main part of the beach that there is a lot of women who have there tits out and only have the nips covered.

"Man, this is heaven," I tell Left. He agrees with me, "man you know that's right."

I see some friends and say what's up to them. We shake hands and keep it pushin. As we get to the basket ball courts I tell Left I need something to drink so I get me some lemonade. He already has his drinking container with what ever he's drinking.

There's all kinds of ladies with there dogs and skaters everywhere. There's even a drum circle. There are a couple of guys saying "can you give me some money for some weed?" We laugh at them and stop some more ladies.

"Hello ladies, do you ladies like jazz?" I ask them. They stop and say "yes we do?" I tell them that we are jazz players and maybe they could come support us some time. The give us big smiles and say sure they would. I ask them there names and they tell us. We tell them our names and Left gets a number and gives out his card.

"Have a good day ladies". They say bye at the same time as they walk off waving. The next girls I see walking toward us has there tits out with the nips covered. I tell Left

"I must know. I got to know".

"Excuse me ladies, my name is Good". They stop and I continue.

"Forgive me for asking but why do you ladies have your twins out today?"

"Well, Good. My name is Felicia and this is Stephanie. We are protesting because men can go topless in public but not women. And it's legal to show the hooter but not the nipple."

"Well ladies I would like to say that you are very beautiful and so are your twins." They give us great big smiles and say in unison "bye" as they wave and walk away.

Left says "Good, you crazy man." We both laugh and slap dap. The rest of the day at the beach went really fast and basically the same. We would get females and try to get numbers from them. Rejection is very much a reality at the beach, but numbers is what it's all about. If you ask 10 ladies for the number, you might go home with about 3 or 4. Depending on how determine you are. It's just a game of cat and mouse.

Females are like very expensive phones. They want to be seen, held, talked to, and touched. But if you push the wrong button, your ass is disconnected.

After the beach adventure, I drop Left off at home and go to the pad. Walking around the beach in the hot sun sure makes you tired. So it's Saturday night and I got to get me some. So before leaving for the jam session, I make a few calls.

I have to call and connect with Denise. She is the lady in red at Baby's Job.

I hit her up and she answers, "Hello."

"Hello Darling, may I speak to Denise please."

She answers, "This is she."

"Hi Denise, this is Good. The guy you met in the lobby yesterday." She says "Oh, I remember you. How are you?"
I answer, "I'm good sweetheart, how you doin?"

She says she is just heading out to meet some friends so I say, "well I don't want to hold you up, I just wanted to say hello and make sure that I did get the right number."

She laughs and says "I don't play games, if I didn't want you to have a number baby; I wouldn't have gave you one at all."

I answer. "Well thank you very much. What's a good time to catch you again?" She says call me anytime, your are more than welcome to call anytime.

"Oh, thank you very much", again I say.

"So I'll call you later darling." She says o.k. and we say our goodbyes and hang up the phone. I then call up Baby.

"Hey Baby, how var you Darling? In my foreign voice. She answers "I'm good sweetheart". "What you doin later I ask her." She says "Why, what's up?"

I tell her that I was thinking of seeing her later on tonight. And she says sure, just call me and let me know. O.k. then I will call you after I come home from a jam session. She says o.k., talk to you later Good. We both say bye and hang up.

I call up Keys and ask him if he needs a ride to the jam session. He tells me "yhea man, cool. Come get me, I'll be ready".

So I get ready for the jam session and take my stuff to the car. Head for Key's place and when I get there I call Keys to let me in and he tells me I will be right back. He had to go to the store right quick. I tell him o.k. I will be waiting in the front of his place.

So there I'm sitting in my car in the front of Keys place and I see a very attractive woman getting her mail out of the boxes. She notice's me looking at her and looks back at me and comes out and say's "Good, is that you?"

I recognize her and say "Yhea, it's me. Tangy, right." I ask.

She says "Yes. How are you?"

I answer, "I'm fine, how are you?"

She says that she is fine and I tell her that I'm waiting for my boy Keys to come back so we can go to a jam session. She says that her sister has her keys and she can't get into there place. I tell her "when Keys comes back, you can wait inside with us. You don't have to wait out here". She says that's very nice of you.

I see Keys pull up and he opens the gate. I tell him that Tangy is waiting for her sister to come home and ask can she wait inside with us in his place. He says sure she can.

So I walk inside the building with Tangy and while were walking down the hall I tell her.

"You remember you said does the cat have any more out there like him. Well I found someone for you".

She says "Oh no, I was just playing."

I said "Me too. I'm talking about me."

She looks at me, pauses and says "But you're trying to talk to my sister."

I tell her "You sister doesn't have time for me. You know what she's up to. I know more about you than I do her."

She agrees and says well your right. I go on to say "I know what school you go to, I know your single and I know you like me." She smiles at me and says "How do you know that?"

I tell her that the way she looked at me when her sister walked me inside there place and what she said.

I also tell her that she had to notice how I could not take my eyes off of her because I thought that she was much prettier than her sister. She just smiles and says o.k.

"You already have the number you can call me."

We sit in Keys place for a little while talking and she went across the hall to see if her sister had came home yet. She comes back and says my sister is home now, thanks for every thing guys. I tell her that I will call her later and walk her to the door.

Keys looks at me and says "Danm, man. She is fine were did you find her?"

I tell him "She is one of your neighbors." We grab his board and head for the jam session. When we get to the jam session everyone is already there and good to go.

We start setting up and tuning up. Sexy walks in and says "Hey fellas". Everyone greets her. She comes up to me and gives me great big hug. Then she goes around and hugs everyone else that she knows as if she didn't want anyone to get jealous.

We introduce her to a couple of other cats and we kick off a really funky groove. She lets the guitar and keyboard get into the groove and then the bass starts in. I stop everyone and say "ok, we need a format. Keys, point at who you want to come in next."

He says o.k. and Sticks counts off the groove. 1,2,3,4. I start playing as to make it a intro so we can really feel the groove.

Sticks plays a fill and we break it down. Keys goes first with a choppy solo. He points at the other sax player and he comes in with some sweet sounding add libs. He points at me and I come in with some burnin riffs that are smokin'. I didn't want the other cat to out do me.

Keys points at Sexy and she come in with some scat vocals. She sounds so good that Keys is just letting her go. And man, can she really go. I come in and out trying to back her up repeating what she is singing. And man it is really sounding sharp.

She loves it and I do too. The other sax guy tries to play some stuff and he sounds terrible. Sticks stops the groove and says "man, dude on the sax is really screwin' the pooch". We all start laughing so hard. Even the sax dude starts laughing too.

"Man, I apologize. I haven't been playing in a long time." He says.

Sticks tells him to try and follow me and what ever I do. He agrees and Sticks kicks off the groove again. 1,2,3,4, everyone comes in and now were really smokin'.

There's a trumpet player that's kinda laid back. He really doesn't say much. He is really a mellow kind of dude. Keys points at him and they break it down and the trumpet player starts in with some fly runs. Then after everyone knows this cat is great, he starts hitting high notes and some of them sound really out of tune and cracking. He stops playing as if he's frustrated and Sticks stops the groove. The trumpet player says "Man, my chops are beat".

"I had a gig earlier today. Sorry fellas." Everyone says "No problem. Don't worry about it. You good."

The rest of the night we had lots of fun. Changed a few grooves and changed solo after solo. I was really impressed with Sexy and don't know why besides she is very sexy and freaky and that I wanted to have her later.

I winked at her several times that evening and she came over and shared the mic with me. I whispered in her ear a few times and finally asked her if she could come by later after the session. She said that sure she could and she would meet me at my place.

After the session, I said my goodbyes and took Keys to the house. I got home expecting to see Sexy there but didn't see her. I called her up on the phone and she said that she had to make a stop and she would be right there. I tell her all right baby and go into the house.

Not to much longer she comes over and she is looking fabulous. She went home to get a change of clothes. I let her in and she says "I hope that you don't mind but I brought a change of clothes".

"Not at all" I answer.

She asks if she could change into something more comfortable. And I tell her yhea baby, take it off.

She goes into the bathroom and changes into a very sexy black baby doll. She comes out of the bathroom and stops in the door way. Her twins are showing from the breast opening and she also has the crotch open.

I tried not to be so excited as I watched her walk closer to me. I turn the lights off and walked over to her. I touched her skin and it was so soft. She smelled so good.

I start undressing in front of her. I took off my shirt first, then my tee-shirt. I kick my shoes off and then unbuckle my belt. She watches me and licks her lips.

I start to dance for her as I was a stripper and she had dollars for me. Off goes my pants and pull down my underwear till you can just see my penis. Then I pull my underwear all the way off and toss them in a chair.

She smiles and says come here daddy. I walk over to her and lean over to kiss her. She grabs me and kisses me. We both moan as if we love it so much.

I tell her she taste good and she tells me my lips are very dangerous. I kiss her on the neck and move down to her breast to lick and suck the nipples. She grinds on my leg and tells me that I am so good with my tongue.

She grabs my penis and starts to stroke it. I touch her pussy and it is so wet and soft.

"Danm baby, you are so wet."

She tells me that I did that to her. She pushes me over and starts to give me some head. I touch her again on her wet warm pussy.

She moans and with the slippery juice from her vagina on my finger, I touch her on her anal opening. She groans and moans louder with my penis in her mouth.

I put two fingers in the pink and one in the stink. Just the tips of my fingers are inside of her and slowly move them in and out. She is going crazy and I can feel her muscles contracting. She loves it and I can tell she is going to cum as she tries to keep sucking my penis.

I slowly play with the openings of her with just the tips of my fingers still and she moans louder and louder. She's grinding and moving faster like she is about to explode in ecstasy. Then she says "Oh, daddy. I'm going to cum. Oh, I'm going to cum.

She tightens up her legs and squeezes her ass together as she screams "I'm cummin baby, I'm cummin baby". Then she locks her legs up and grabs me tight fisted. "Good, Good, Good", she cries out.

I know she is sassyfied, so now I move in for the kill. I climb on top of her as she tells me "Get some Daddy. Tear it up baby", she says. I put the head in and she opens her mouth as if she is opening her pussy.

"Oh, you're so big" she tells me. I ease the rest of me slowly into her wet, warm pussy. She starts with the oooohhhs and aaaaaahhhs. I start to stroke her slowly in and out. Then I begin to ride her like the rodeo show.

"Yhea, baby. This pussy is so good" I tell her. She tells me back "It's yours daddy. That's your pussy. Get it, get it good."

Harder and faster I go. Faster and harder. She tries to grab my ass as I ride her. Deeper and harder. She's screaming now "Oh Good, Oh Good" and got me moaning too.

"Ooh yhea baby, mmmmm, yhea, yhea," we exchange yes sounds as we both cum together.

"Aaaawwww, yeessss, ooohhh, aaaahhh".

We both stop and stare each other in the eyes. We both agree that it was so, so good. I rub her arms up and down as she rubs my back up and down. I feel light headed and she tells me "You drive me crazy". We lay there for a moment and before you know it we are both in a deep sleep together.

Chapter Eight

The next morning, I wake up and kiss her on the forehead. "Hey Sexy, wake up" I say to her.

She opens her eyes and says hi. I ask her if she slept well. She says "I sure did, what time is it"? I look at the clock and tell her its 8 o'clock in the morning. She says oh o.k. I gonna get up in a little bit.

I get out of the bed and jump in the shower. She comes into the bathroom and jumps into the shower with me. I kiss her and start to wash her back side and she washes mine. She washes my penis and it jumps right to attention.

She says "Oh my".

She washes my balls and I start sucking her tities. Right there in the shower I bend her over and slide inside of her doggy style. She puts her hands up on the tile and I start pounding her from behind. I grab her hair and pull it back as if I was riding a horse.

She loves it. "Get it daddy" she says. "Oh Good, beat it up". She tells me.

I'm beating it up and slapping her on the ass at the same time. She screams in pleasure as we exchange the yes sounds again. I pull out of her and bust a fat one her ass.

I rub my penis against her ass like I'm rubbing my cum into her ass, like it was lotion or something.

"Danm baby, you bring out the best in me" I tell her. She laughs and says "you mean I bring the best out of you". We laugh together as I wash myself up.

I exit the shower to dry off and she finishes washing herself off too. I put on some underwear and a robe and go into the kitchen.

I pull out all of my ingredients for the gumbo and put them on the table. I go back into the bedroom and she is getting dressed. I start to get dressed too. After we are both dressed she tells me that she will see me later and I agree that I will call her later.

She says "I will leave you with your boys today. I know how you guys are with your sports".

I kiss her and open the door for her. She kisses me on her way out the door and I slap her on the ass really hard as she leaves out. Goodbye Sexy I tell her before I close the door.

I head back to the kitchen to get the gumbo started. I start chopping up all the vegetables with my mini chopper. And the phone rings. I answer the phone, "Hello". I hear a sweet sexy voice "Hello, can I please speak to Good".

"This is he, who is this" I ask.

She says this is Alize. "Oh, hi Alize. How are you"?

"I'm fine" she says. I tell her "I didn't think that you were going to call me."

She says "I aint missin out on your gumbo. I love me some gumbo." We both laugh it up.

"So what time should I come by"? She asks.

"How about around 4 o'clock". I tell her.

She says "That's fine, so where am I coming". I tell her "I hope that you're cumming between your legs". And we both start cracking up some more.

And then she says "I mean what's your address Mr. Good"?

I give her my address and tell her that I have to get back to the kitchen. She says o.k. and we say our goodbyes.

I clean the chicken up and chop it into cubes. Then I put on the gumbo and start to chop up the sausage and clean the shrimp and crab.

After everything is finished being prepared, I start on the rue. I make sure the skillet is very hot first. I put some shortening into a skillet and start to sprinkle some flour into it after it gets hot.

I mix in some paprika, thyme, salt and pepper and make sure that I stir because I don't want it to burn. If the rue burns, your gumbo aint gone be shit. It will taste burnt and very nasty like burnt toast soup.

After my rue was ready, I slowly poured it into the gumbo. This is very dangerous because the rue is very hot like lava and it boils like a volcano when it hits the gumbo stock.

Pouring and stirring, I mix it all together and then add my sausage. It really is starting to smell like gumbo now and the shrimp and crab is the last thing to go in.

I clean my rice and let a big giant pot of rice simmer while the gumbo is simmering also. After about 35 to 45 minutes I add the seafood. And stir it all in together.

The phone rings and I answer it. Its Left, he says he is on his way. "Cool man, I will see you in a few."

I hang up the phone. Checking on the gumbo, it really smells good. I give it little taste and man does it taste good. It all comes together.

The door bell rings and I answer the door. It's Lil Mama,

"Hey Lil Mama, come on in." She comes in and gives me a great big hug.

"Man, I miss you" she says. I tell her that I miss her too. We go into the kitchen and she says, "Danm, it smells good in here" and then ask "is it ready"? I tell her it's just about ready, just a little longer.

She says well I'm ready. Come on good. I tell her that I'm tired and she laughs and says yhea, I'll do all the work. Pulls me into the front room and walks me over to the couch. She sits down on the couch and pulls me close to her, unzips my pants and takes out my penis. She starts licking the head and sucking me.

Lil Mama is very talented in this department. She sucks and strokes me at the same time knowing that what she does will make any man cum really fast. She is a professional.

She moans and groans as if she loves it turning her head side to side.

The door rings and I tell her to hold on a second. She says no, they can wait and keeps on sucking. She is so good at it that I can not hold it and she makes me cum in her mouth.

Pow, I bust a nut and she takes all of it. As if she is trying to punish me. I pull away and tell her danm Lil Mama. You aint nothin nice. As I walk to the door and ask "who is it"? They answer, "Its Quick man, let me in".

I open the door holding up my pants and he says "Man I hope I didn't interrupt anything" with a smile on his face. I tell him no, not at all and to come right in.

He walks in and see's Lil Mama sitting on the couch. "Hey Lil Mama" he says. He is no stranger to this sex-a-holic.

She says "Hey Quick, come here baby". She gives him a rubber from out of her purse and takes him to the bed room. I go to the bathroom to wipe my dick off and the doorbell rings again. Ding dong.

I answer the door and its Sticks and Keys.

"Hey fellas, come on in. You're just in time," I tell them. Sticks says, "Man it sure smells good in here". I tell him I been slavin in the kitchen all morning.

He asks, "Is the game on yet" and I tell him I don't know I was a little occupied with someone he knows. He ask me who and I tell him "Lil Mama. She's got Quick in the room right now."

"Word" they both say at the same time. Then all of the sudden you can hear ooh's and aah's coming out of the bed room. "Man, Quick is killin it". Keys says. Keys starts for the bedroom door.

"I'm going to see what's happening. He opens the door, walks right in and shuts the door behind him.

Lil Mama is happy to see Keys and Quick is getting that ass from behind. Keys goes over to her and zips his pants down. Pulls out his dick and gives it to Lil Mama. She loves it and starts sucking it while Quick hits it from behind Doggy Style.

Sticks tells me while were waiting outside of the bedroom that he wants to see what's going on in the room. So I go and open the door and show him.

"Look man, she taking it from two at one time. She looks at us both, pulls Keys dick out of her mouth and says "Sticks, get over here and gimmi some of what you got".

Sticks goes over and stands right by her and she grabs his pants with one hand while sucking Keys. Unbuckles his pants and zips down his zipper. Now she has Keys on one side, Sticks on the other side and Quick hittin it from the back. Man, it's a three way gang bang and she is loving it.

She is moaning and groaning and switching from the left side to the right. She jacks off one dick as she sucks the other then switches and does the same on the other side. Quick get his nut and pulls out of the pussy.

Keys jumps behind her and starts on her doggy style. Now she has both of them at the same time. One in the front and one in the back. They go on for about a few more minutes and they cum almost at the same time. She is just moanin and groanin and giving up those yes sounds.

"Yes, yes, yes, fuck me, fuck me, cum for me daddy". They back off of her and get there selves together, wipe themselves off and everyone is sitting in the front room now. Laid back and watching the TV.

Lil Mama comes out of the room but ass naked and stands on the coffee table and says, "Is that all yall got."

"Get them dicks workin". I bust up laughin and go over to her and slap her on the ass. The game is on so I tell her that we want to watch the game now. I know that they probably have to recuperate.

I ask them "Who's hungry"? Everyone says "me" at the same time. I tell them to wash there nasty ass hands before they come into the kitchen.

I head to the kitchen and break out the bowls and spoons. I tell them to help there selves and everyone is getting there eat on.

Man, this is the bomb, Keys says and everyone agrees. Lil Mama is sucking on some crab legs and Quick says, "Danm, Lil Mama, you wasn't sucking me like that. And everyone starts laughing really hard. Even Lil Mama.

"Who wants something to drink" I ask. I hear "Me".

Keys says "What you got".

I tell them "I got Coke, Orange, Corona and MGD." They tell me 3 Corona's and 2 Cokes.

I get up and go into the kitchen and bring back the drinks. Left says "I want to give a toast". He holds up his beer and says "To good times". We all hold our drinks up and give the toast.

Everyone finishes the food and we are all kicking back watching the game. Everyone is shouting and getting excited cause the game is exciting.

"Interception" I holler.

Quick says "There he goes. He just may go all the way". Sticks says, "Look at him go". "He's at the 50, the 40, the 20, the 10, Touchdown"!

We all scream and I get up and start dancing. I grab Lil Mama and pull her up and dance her around the place. Everyone is laughing and havin a great time.

Sticks says, "You kill me man, the way you're always clownin around". I tell him I just like to have a good time. Life is short.

We watch the rest of the game and turn to the next game that is on that day. Everyone is feeling good and full and faded.

Talking shit is very much part of having fun, as we all are talking big shit to each other.

Time passes by and a few of the guys eat again and so does Lil Mama. Keys could never hold his liquor so only a few beers are getting him drunk.

After his third one he is really acting up. So Sticks says man I got to get Keys home I think he's had enough fun for today. He's leaning on people as he talks right in front of there face. Lil Mama pushes his face away from hers and says "nigga, yo breath stank". Everyone bust up laughing as he stumbles away from her.

Sticks grabs his shirt and puts his arm around Keys and says "tell everyone goodbye man. It's time to go". They say good bye and head out the door.

As I watch them walk out I notice a car pull up and I looks like Alize getting out of the car. She walks around the car and I can see that it is her. I give her a holla. "Hey baby" I shout at her. She looks at me and gives me the prettiest smile.

"Come on in baby" I tell her. She walks up looking very sexy with some tight jeans on and a sexy ass top, showing off her breast and small waist. I hold my hand out to help her inside the door. She steps over the door step with her high heels on and I tell her "You look very nice today cutie".

She smiles some more and I tell her "Welcome to my Casa."

"Come one in and make yourself at home."

I introduce her to Lil Mama first and then go around the place. "This is Lil Mama, Lil Mama this is Alize". They say hello to each other.

"These guys are my good friends Left and Quick. Fellas this is Alize".

They both say hello looking at her like she was the next entrée because she is so fine. I ask her if she is ready to eat and she says "You know I am, I been waiting all day for this".

So I give her a bowl and tell her to help herself. I show her where the rice and gumbo is and tell her don't be shy. I want you to really enjoy yourself. She says thank you. I ask her if she wants something to drink, I have Coke, Orange, Corona, and MGD. She says, "I'll have a MGD". I get her a beer out the fridge and we sit at the table in the kitchen.

I ask her if she likes football and she tells me not really. "I just came for the gumbo."

"So you didn't want to see me," I ask. She says "Well, I do think you're cute". I tell her that I think she is really beautiful also and she gives me a really pretty smile.

I tell her don't think I invite a lot of women here to eat my food. I wanted to get to know you and it seemed like an opportunity at the time when I saw you in the store. It just kinda happened this way.

She says, I was thinking about that and goes on to say I don't really take numbers at work either. She looks at me and says "don't think I'm easy, I'm not easy".

I tell her that nothing worth while comes easy and give her a big smile with it. She smiles back and I ask her if she likes the gumbo.

She says, "yhea, sure, this is good Mr. Good."

The fellas holla in the other room and I get up and tell her I'll be right back.

"Touchdown" everyone shouts. I look at the score and walk back into the kitchen and Alize is getting her grub on. She really likes it I can see. I sit back down with her and ask her so how long have you been working at the store? She tells me around 2 months. So that's why I have never seen you before.

She tells me that she lives around the corner from the store and just happened to find a job there. I ask her if she likes jazz. She says yhea sure. I tell her that I play in a band and she says that would explain all the music stuff all around your place. I smile and say "yhea, I'm kind of a collector when it comes to musical instruments".

She asks me how many instruments do I have and I tell her "Well about 9. I have 4 saxophones, 2 keyboards, some congas, a trumpet and a EWI".

She says what is a EWI? I tell her it's an electronic wind instrument. She looks confused so I explain. I blow into the mouthpiece and electronic sounds comes out of it like synth sounds, different horns, strings, what ever I turn it to. She says Oh, o.k. I see.

You know you look like a musician you know. I laugh and say to her "what does that mean"? She says, "I mean you look very creative". Ok, I answer. That's cool.

"So, you know I'm gonna ask you if you have a boyfriend."

She says, "If I did, I wouldn't be over here". I tell her well some things you never know.

I reach over the table and hold her hand as I touch her wedding ring finger. "You ever been married" I ask. She says almost, it was almost a terrible mistake. He didn't respect me. He tried to hit me one day and that was it. I had to go. I don't deal with no crazy ass man.

I laugh and tell her "I don't blame you. It's some crazy ass niggas out here". She laughs and we smile at each other. I let her eat as I look into her eyes and enjoy her beauty in my presence. She sees me kinda smiling at her and says why are you smiling so much. I tell her that it is a satisfied smile and I am very satisfied with her company.

She smiles at me and says you sure know what to say to a girl to make her smile. I tell her I love to see her smile. She tells me "You know you never asked me for my number. Why"?

I tell her I don't know, it just seemed like you were letting me know that you were interested enough for me to let you give it to me without asking. But I wasn't going to let you walk out of here today without giving it to me. And she says what if I don't want you to have it. I just want to call you.

I look at her like she just ripped my heart in two. And she laughs and says I'm just kidding. I wasn't leaving without giving it to you. I want you to have it. I think we are going to be good friends. I can just tell she says.

Me too I answer. I get up from the table and walk around to her side and give her a kiss on the cheek. She smiles and says you better watch those hot lips. I tell her I rather watch you with yo fine self and walk into the front room to find out the score.

I try not to leave her in the kitchen by herself for too long but the game is good and it is tied score.

She finishes her food, puts her bowl into the sink and comes into the front room. I tell her I'm sorry this is a good game. I tell Left to scoot over so she can sit down and she tells me to sit there first. I sit down and she comes over and sits on my lap. I can smell her hair and it smells so good.

I get excited and I know she can feel the bulge in my pants poking her. She has a really nice plump ass and I have my hands on her thighs caressing them slowly. I look over at Lil Mama and she winks at me.

Lil Mama thinks she is pretty and gives me the "You go boy" wink.

The Saints score a field goal and win the game. We all shout in a joyous voice. "Yhea baby, Yhea. Man that was a good game" Left says.

Quick says "Man, dem Saints gone to da SuperBowl Again". "Who Dat" he shouts out loud.

Left says "Alright yall, I got to go. Man Good, thanks for everything man."

Lil Mama says "Can you give me a ride to the crib?" Left tells her sure Lil Mama, come on lets go."

"Bye Good," Lil Mama says as she gets up and walks to the door.

"Everything was great; we must do this again fellas." And gives us a warm smile as if we know what she's talking about and we do.

Quick says "I got to go too and winks at me." He don't want to cock block either so he gets up and heads for the door. I tell everyone that I'll see them later and thanks for coming.

They tell me thanks for everything and the gumbo was the bomb. They all walk out the door and I shut the door and start over toward Alize.

She looks at me and says why you looking at me like that. You better not try nothing. I laugh and get closer to her as I touch her legs and she jumps up I try to grab her. She starts to run away from me and I start with my vampire voice.

"I want to suck your blood" I tell her.

She runs away laughing and I chase her.

"Come here" I shout at her chasing her around the couch. I corner her by a chair and grab her as she screams stop. We wrestle a little bit and I end up on top of her looking her in her wanting eyes.

I stare at her for a moment as she stares back at me. I move slowly toward her lips, closer and closer. Our noses meet and I rub my nose against hers. She asks me "what am I doing?"

And I tell her "let me show you."

I kiss her slowly as she doesn't even try to pull back away from me. She kisses me back and we go into a wet, warm, and passionate kiss.

She starts to caress me all over and I caress her back. I touch her hair, face, arms, legs, back and squeeze her ass.

I then gently touch one of her breast and she starts to moan. I try to unbutton her shirt and she says no, we shouldn't be doing this. She then sits up and pushes me away at the same time.

I ask her what is wrong and she says you're not going to respect me if we do this. I know she is right, so I sit there and say nothing.

She looks at me and says, "I want to give you something to look forward to."

I tell her that if she doesn't feel comfortable with it then we should think about it and relax. I sit back and grab the remote to change the channel. She scoots closer to me and says "I'm sorry; I just don't want to seem easy because I know that you won't respect me later".

I tell her "It's cool baby, we can take our time and you can have as much time as you like."

She smiles and says that's what I'm talking about. I took you for a different type of guy. Someone that was just out to get some booty.

"Alize", I say. "I don't even know you like that yet. I really don't know why I kissed you. I barley even know you. You could have some kind of health issue's or something."

She looks at me and says "What the hell are you talking about". I cut her off and say "I didn't mean it like that. I meant that you can't be too careful now days". She looks like her feelings are hurt and tells me "You aint ready for this anyway, you probably can't handle this".

I know that she is jumping on the defensive side. So I go along with it and tell her that she is the one not ready and she can't handle me. She goes on and on about who can handle who and how much of a woman she is. So I tell her if she wants to bet we can play a game.

Chapter Nine

She says what game and I tell her it's called "Cum for me Boo". She asks me how do you play that. I tell her that we see who can make the other person cum the most.

"When you are ready to play I will show you who can handle who". She agrees and says you'll see who can handle who. I tell her we will just have to see then.

I can tell that this is a woman that likes to argue and get her way. So I back off and start up something else.

"So did you really like the gumbo or what"? She looks at me and says that the gumbo was really good and that she would like to take some home. I tell her that she can eat all she wants to but she can not take anything home.

I don't let food leave the house. She says that she is full right now and that maybe she might eat again later. So I ask her if she would like to watch a movie. She says sure and I go over to the DVD rack and pull out some of the latest movies.

I start reading the movies and she stops me at a girly movie. So I put in the girly movie just to be nice and we watch it for awhile. I am really board with this movie so I start to dose off by the middle of the movie.

She is sitting next to me and I am leaning over on her, lying on her shoulder. She pulls my head down and puts it on her lap and tells me to kick my feet up. So I do and tell her that I'll just nap for a minute.

While I'm lying on her lap she is caressing my head and face. Playing in my hair she bends over and kisses me. I wake and turn as to face her lying on my back.

Now I'm looking at her and she's looking at me. She bends her head down and kisses me again and we start to kiss passionately and slowly. I tell her that she better stop because she knows were this is going to end up. She tells me its o.k. I'm a big girl and I can handle myself.

She then tells me "So how do you play this game again". I sit up and tell her "come, let's go into the bedroom boo".

I get up off the couch and grab her hand. We walk into the bedroom holding hands and I kiss her at the foot of the bed. She starts to unbuckle my pants and unzip the zipper. I unbutton her blouse and unfasten her bra. She tells me "wait" and I stand there as she takes her jeans off. We both finish undressing.

She comes over to me and tells me so who is going to be first? I tell her ladies first and lay her down on the bed as I climb on top of her.

Kissing her lips slowly, I move down to her neck. She starts to hum. Mmmmmmm, that feels good she says. Then I move to her breast and slowly lick and suck around the nipples. She puts her hands around my head and lets me suck each of breasts slow and long. Licking the nipple soft and gently biting them one at a time. Then I suck as much as I can put into my mouth. In and out and then concentrating on the nipple.

She sounds like she loves it. I hear the yes sounds.

"Mmmmmmm, yes baby. That feels so good she says."

I touch her pussy and it is wet and warm. I slowly slide my finger around clit being careful not to touch it first. Down and around the wetness of her pussy, I slowly put the tip of my finger into her opening to get some of her juices on my finger.

She sighs "Oh, Good". I then use the wetness of her pussy to search for her clit.

With her pussy juice on the tip of my finger I slide it over her protruding clit. She again tells me it feels good. So I rub my finger around it and across it.

It is driving her wild as I ask her "Do you like that".

She says yes. And I tell her to "cum for me boo".

She says o.k. and I enter inside her with my finger. First half way and then all of my finger and yes she is very tight. She is moaning and telling me oh, that feels good baby.

I tell her "Cum for me boo, cum for me".

She starts to grind and moan and groan. Oooohhh, Good. Mmmmmm, baby.

I start to finger her a little faster and deeper trying to touch her clit with my thumb at the same time. She's getting louder and more and more excited.

"Yes baby, yes baby" she says.

I use a third finger to slide close to her booty hole and she gets really exited.

I'm sliding my finger inside her. My thumb is touching her clit and my lower finger is touching her booty hole. This is driving her wild and she is going crazy saying my name and clinching my neck with one hand and clinching the bed with the other.

I tell her "yes baby, yes."

She answers me with "yes baby uh ha."

I start to tell her over and over, "Cum for me boo". I repeat this over and over several times till she comes all over my hand and screams with joy.

"Yes baby, I'm Cuming, I'm Cuming."

"Oooooooohhhhhhh shit, yes baby." As I tell her "cum on boo, cum on boo". I slowly pull my fingers away from her soft wet pussy and tell her thank you for Cuming for me. She laughs and says "No, thank you boo".

She pulls me toward her and turns me over to lay me on my back. Places her hands on my dick and starts to stroke it. Up and down she says "Yhea boo, now it's your turn."

She climbs on top of me and slides my hard dick inside of her slowly. I moan "oooohhh yhea boo" and she is very wet and warm.

I start to grind inside of her and she grinds back. The pussy is so tight and the friction is causing me to tell her "ooh baby you're so tight, danm it's so good". She says cum for me boo and starts to grind faster.

I grab her ass with both hands and stat to hump a little faster. We both listen to each other moan and groan.   "Mmmmm, oooooohhh, aaaaaaahhhh, mmmmmm."

I lift her ass up in the air with both hands on her cheeks and start to pound harder from under her. Uhm, uhm, uhm, I let her feel me with every stroke as I pull almost all the way out and shove it all the way in with force. She starts to get louder and louder.

Cum for me boo she screams, cum for me. And I start to reach my climax, stronger and stronger. She is also climaxing as she says "Oh baby I'm going to cum again".

I'm telling her to cum and she's telling me to cum and almost at the same time we both explode together.

"Oohh, baby, ooooh, mmmmm, yeeesss, uh ha, uh ha, uuuuuhhhh".

She stops grinding and I slow down to almost a dead stop slowly pushing and pulling my dick in and out of her. I push it all the way in one last time and she screams oohh baby.

Then I pull all the way out and tell her to let me up. She says no not yet and kisses me a few more times. I roll her over and kiss her a few more times. I tell her that was so good baby. And she agrees by nodding her head slowly.

I don't believe that this is my third nut today as I stagger and fall over on the bed breathing tiredly. She gets up and says I'll get you a warm towel. Goes into the bath room and turns on the water. She comes back after a few moments with a warm towel and wipes my penis and balls off.

I think to myself, this is a caring woman who goes and gets me a towel and cleans me off. I lay there and ask her if she's going to leave soon because I want to take a nap. She says that she wants some more gumbo so I tell her make yourself at home and eat all you want I was going to take a quick nap. She says o.k. and I roll ever but naked and fall asleep.

When I wake up about two hours later, I put on some underwear and look out of the bedroom. She is sitting in the front room watching TV, stretched out across the couch.

"Hey Good, how was your nap baby"? She asks me. "It was good baby" I answer. She gets up and gives me a great big hug and kisses me on the neck.

"I am having such a good time here with you". She says "I know you trust me because no man that just met me would have left me in there place while they sleep. I could have robbed you or killed you or anything".

I thought about it as she said it and thought, man, she is absolutely right. I must have been out of my mind.

I tell her that I know were she works. I am exhausted still so I sit on the couch and asked her did she eat all the gumbo she laughs and says no. I couldn't have eaten all that gumbo in there. She comes over to the couch and sits beside me and tells me to lay my head on her. So I do and we sit there and she flips the channels and asks me what I want to watch. I tell what ever is fine.

She rubs my head ever so slowly like I was her pet. She start talking about if I really like her and that she really likes me a lot. But deep inside me I know that she was just something that happened and she will probably, most likely not end up as my one and only girl.

So I let her go on and on and then I tell her that we are both adults and we know what we want. I tell that we can be good friends for now and just see if it takes us anywhere else. I tell her to come close so I can give her a kiss and tell her that she is a very special friend, near and dear to me. She smiles and kisses me back.

We watch TV for a while and I tell her that I have to go over Keys place to go over some new material. I really didn't have to go over Keys place. I just told her that to get rid of her. She says o.k. and starts to get herself together.

When she is ready to go, I give another great big hug and walk her to the door. She gives me one last kiss as I open the door and I tell her don't be a stranger.

"Call me anytime". She walks out the door and turns to give me one more kiss. I tell her to call me and let me know that she made it home. She walks away and I close the door.

Man, what a day today. I think to myself. I am exhausted so I go back to lie on the couch for a little while. I get up and go into the kitchen and put up the food. I look in the sink and all the dishes are clean to my surprise. Alize washed and put all the dishes up.

WOW. I am shocked. Well she aint no lazy bitch, that's for sure. I go into the bedroom and get my robe off of the door. I go back into the front room and kick back on the couch in my robe. I dose off and fall into a deep sleep with the TV watching me.

I wake up the next morning and man, am I hungry. I go into the kitchen to fix me something to eat and open the fridge. Take out some eggs and some rice and butter. Grab a skillet and make me good old fashion rice and egg. I sit at the table eating my rice and egg and the phone rings.

"Hello", I answer the phone.

"Man, what's good with you Good". Says Left.   "Hey Left" I answer back.

"You still got any gumbo left", he ask me.

"Sure, I got a half a pot left man. You better come by and get some more man", I tell him.

He says, "I'm on my way man. I'll be there in a few minutes. Don't leave".

He hangs up the phone and I do also. I jump into the shower after I finish my food. After the shower I get some clothes on and go into the kitchen to clean up the dishes. The door rings and I go to answer the door. It's Left.

"Come on in man. You know were everything is. Help yourself man".

I turn on the TV and flip through a few channels. I end up landing on a sports game and we talk about yesterday.

"Man Good, you sure know how to show people a good time" says Left.

"I try my best Sir" I reply. Left says, Lil Mama aint no joke. She was right on time man. I laugh and tell him yhea she had us all feelin right. He ask me do I give her favors or money or something and I tell him no, not at all. She just likes to fuck and suck man.

165

She's a real nymphomaniac. She doesn't care where, when or how. She just loves dick. Fat, skinny, short or long, she just loves them. She does use condoms though. At least I can say she is clean.

We sit around shootin the shit and watchin the tube for a little while and left says alright man. That was good. You sure know that gumbo man.

I think about Baby and wonder if she would like some gumbo. So I call her up. The phone rings and she answers, "Hello". I say Hello Baby, how are you darling? She says Hi Good, I'm fine. How are you?

I tell her that I'm good, always good. She laughs. I say "Look, I have some gumbo that I made, would you like some"? She says "Hell yhea, I want some gumbo. I tell her that I'll bring it right over and ask her what she is doing today.

She says nothing just cleaning my place up and getting ready for my week. I tell her I'll be over in a few hours. I will call her before I come. She says ok, I will look forward to seeing you in a little while. And we both say goodbye and hang up the phones.

Left says who was that and I tell him it was Baby. A lady that I met some time ago and that she is a really beautiful person. I show him a picture of her and he shouts, "Supermurgitroid". I ask him if he likes her picture and he says "Hell yhea, she is fine. Danm, Good. You the man, she is just too much".

We sit around a little while longer watching the game and talking shit to each other.

I think about Tangy, Keys neighbor and ask him about her. Hey man, have you seen Tangy around? He says no, man. I aint seen her since you brought her by that day.

So I call her up and see how she's doing. The phone rings a few times and someone answers.

"Hello. I answer back.

"Hello, can I speak to Tangy"?

A voice says who's speaking. I say it's Good. The voice says aint you supposed to asking for me, what the hell is going on, and gives the phone to Tangy. "Hello" Tangy says and I can hear all kinds of yelling in the back ground. Hey Tangy, how are you sweetie. She says I'm good. I just don't think that it's a good time to talk right now. I'm going to call you back in a little while, I have to talk to Tonya. I tell her o.k. and say make sure you call me back, I have something for you. She says o.k. and we hang up the phone.

After the game I tell Left I have to make a run. He says ok Good. Thanks for everything man and heads for the door. Later man I tell him. Peace out Good, he answers back

Chapter Ten

Later on, I fix Baby a bowl of gumbo and put some rice in a separate container. I call her up and tell her that I'm on my way and she says o.k. I can't wait. See you when you get here. And we hang up and I head for the ride. I get to my car and head for Baby's place. As I'm driving to Baby's place the phone rings and its Sexy.

"Hi Good", she says.

"Hey Sexy", I answer back.

"What you doing today" she asks me. I tell her that I aint doing too much what's up with you. She says I wanted to treat you to a movie. Oh, really I answer. She says yhea, I really like you and I wanted to treat you to a movie. I say o.k. so I'm making a run right now, I will call you back in a little while. She says o.k. and we say our goodbyes.

I get to Baby's place and tell her that I'm outside; she says o.k. and tells me to come on in. I get out of the car, grab her food and head for Baby's door.

As I'm walking down the hallway I can hear someone yelling and shouting. It's getting louder and louder as I walk down the hall. I stop at Baby's door and the shouting is kind of loud and I wonder is it coming out of Baby's place and all of the sudden I hear a crash and some slapping and screaming.

I aint the smartest person in the world but it sounds like someone is getting there ass kicked. I hear a male voice saying "You bitch, I told you". The woman's voice is saying "Stop, please stop, please".

I knock on the door and Baby opens the door. "Hey Good" she says, come on in. I tell her that one of her neighbors is getting there ass kicked and she says that they always fighting over there, All day and night sometimes.

I hand over her goods and she says thank you so very much Good. I love gumbo. She tells me to have a seat and goes right into the kitchen to warm up her food. She says I hope you don't mind but I'm hungry man. I tell her no, not at all. Go right ahead and enjoy yourself.

I watch what ever she has on the TV because it is interesting. I ask her what the hell are you watching and she says "Faces of Death". I tell her oh, o.k. I've seen this be fore. And she tells me that they have a new version.

She comes out of the kitchen with her gumbo and sits at her table and says don't mind me. I'm getting my grub on baby. I tell her to enjoy and she starts tearing it up. Mmmmmm, this is so good. Thanks you so much Good. I just sit there and smile as she eats her food.

After she finishes her food she comes over and sits by me. Gives me a great big hug and kiss and says "You are definitely the marrying type". I laugh and say you are too. I tell her that maybe one day we will go to Las Vegas and go to a drive thru wedding chapple and order us a number 2 special. She laughs and gives me a kiss on the lips.

She gets up and puts a movie in and says can you stay awhile. I tell her that sure I can. So we sit there hugged up and cuddling on her couch, as we watch some movie that she put in. I really don't pay to much attention to the movie because she is so beautiful.

I realize that she may be the one. I mean the one that I may be with for the rest of my life. You know, hang up my players' card and grow old together with.

She talks about the movie and I answer back to keep her attended to. I try, but I can't keep my hands to myself. I touch her hair and stroke it. It is so soft. I touch her arms, ears and skin slowly. Her skin is so soft. I keep thinking about how much of a great time we had together when we made love. Well at the time I guess it was just sex, but it was great either way.

I ask her if she can cook and she answers "yhea baby. One day I will cook for you". One way that I can tell if someone can cook is to ask them how do you cook rice? If you can cook rice you can cook anything. If you cook rice out of a box then most likely you can't cook. If it comes out of a bag, you have to clean it by washing it out to get rid of the starch. Then you have to let it boil and just as it begins to boil then you have to turn the fire down and let it simmer for about 20 minutes. If you can do this that you can cook.

Just to test her I ask her what is the number one rule of cooking? She says I don't know, what is the number one rule of cooking? I tell her that the number one rule of cooking is to never leave the kitchen. And we both laugh so hard out loud.

I remember that I had made plans with Sexy, she wanted to treat me to a movie. So I make up something that could get me out of her place. Hey Baby, I have to go to a meeting about a gig that we have coming up soon. She says o.k. what time are you coming back she ask me. I tell her that I don't really know. I can call you when I think I'm coming back and she says ok Good. Call me later and come back by. I want to spend some time with you. I tell her ok beautiful, I will see you later baby.

I get up and break for the door almost forgetting to kiss her goodbye so she reminds me. Good, aren't you forgetting something she says. I look at her and she's walking toward me and I remember. Those sweet, sexy, luscious lips.

I grab her around her waist and pull her to me. Look her deep in her eyes and tell her kiss me darling in my foreign voice. She looks at me and says, "Yes darling" imitating me in a foreign voice. We kiss slowly, gently. She is a very good kisser and so am I.

I get excited and my pants starts to poke out at her. She says oh, so you like. I tell her very much, I do, I do, I do. She laughs and tells to hurry back my love as we were in a love story. That's when it hit me. That word. Love. She said it and I felt it when she said it. Could it be that I'm falling in love with her. I wonder. If I was, would I let myself go with it or would I run from it as fast as I could.

I walk out of the door and think about it as I walk to the car. Love, far as I could remember. Love was just a four letter word that meant nothing. My definition was two fools with a misunderstanding. That's what I thought about love. I mean I love a lot of things, but not any of my women. I always made sure that I could walk away from any relationship if I had too in minutes flat. Trust no bitch was my motto. Money over hoes. Pimps up and hoes down.

They all had me tuff as nails and I thought I would never bend the rules, not even for a second. And here I am thinking about this lady as if she had my heart in her hand. Was she a heart breaker? Was I falling in love with this beautiful girl? I played some Marvin Gay on the way to Sexy's place to get me in the mood. I had to get Baby off my mind. This was not normal. So I sang Marvin Gay's "Let's get it on".

I get to Sexy's place and think, I didn't even call he to let her know that I was coming over. So I call her from the front of her place. She answers the phone and tells me that she is ready she will be right out.

She comes out a few minutes later and we drive off to the movies. I ask her what does she want to see and she says that it's a really good movie out called Frankie and Alice. We get to the movie theater and park the car and she says to me wait, can I have a kiss. I lean over to kiss her and we kiss. She says thank you and we get out of the car and walk into the theater.

We stand in line to get the tickets and when we get to the ticket counter the sales person ask may I help you. She says yes can we have two tickets for Frankie and Alice. The sales person says that will be 22 dollars. Sexy gets some money out of her purse and slides the money under thru the window. The sales lady passes the tickets and change back thru the window and tells us to enjoy the show.

We walk inside and hand the tickets to the door person. He tells us theater number 6 is to your right. Sexy ask me if I want any thing from the concession stand and I tell her no. I'm good, Thank you. She says that she wants some popcorn so we stand in line to get her pop corn.

She won't let me pay for the popcorn and I smile at her and say you are so sweet. She gets her change and I carry her drink for her as we go to the end of the counter to put some butter on the popcorn.

She is putting a lot of butter on the popcorn so I say "wow, you sure are putting a lot of butter on there". She says that she likes a lot of butter on her popcorn. I grab a lot of napkins for her because she is going to need a lot of napkins with all that butter.

We head for the theater and I tell her "here it is babe, right hear" and open the door for her. We go inside of a dark movie theater and there are plenty seats everywhere. I ask her where does she want to sit and she says lets go up to the top. So we climb all the way up to the top and are the only two up that far. We sit down and she starts moving arm rest up and tells me to give her the soda. She puts it in a cup holder on the other side of her, and starts to munch on the popcorn. She asks me if I want some and I tell her no thank you.

The previews are one and we watch some of the previews and talk about what is going to be good. They always make the previews look good. So a few more people come into the theater and sit about six rows down from us. There are only about a dozen people in the theater tonight spread all around the place but we are the only two up at the top.

The place dims even darker and the movie screen gets shorter. The movie starts and she tells me to let her have another kiss. She kisses me passionately and touches my face with her clean hand that she was holding the popcorn box with. We sit there and watch the movie for a little while and about 30 minutes later she leans over to me and says now I'm going to give you your treat I was telling you about.

I thought that the movie was the treat so I look at her and wait in anticipation. She puts the popcorn down and leans over to kiss me again.

This time she grabs my pants and unfastens them. She finds my zipper and unzips my pants. Puts her hand inside of my pants and touches my penis. I ask her what are you doing and she tells me "nothing. Shhhh, be quiet".

I relax and let her go on with what ever she is trying to do. It doesn't take long before I am excited with a hard on and she is jacking me off right there in the movie theater. She leans over to me and says you want some butter for your popcorn. Then she takes her hand and puts it in the popcorn tub and touches my dick with her buttery fingers. I kinda feels good and so I tell her "ooh, that feels good baby".

She can tell that I like it because my dick is really hard now. She strokes me with her buttery hands and I'm looking to make sure that no one is looking and they don't have a clue that we are doing this right in the theater.

Everyone has there eyes on the screen in front of them. Sexy leans over and kisses my dick and puts it right in her mouth. Giving me head right there in the movie theater. I just lean back and scoot down in the seat. She tells me that the butter taste good and sucks and slurps and then I tell her "sshhh be quiet".

She quiets down and strokes me at the same time that she gives me head and I think I'm going to come. I grab the back of her neck and rub her on the back and then she starts really licking, sucking and jacking me off all at the same time. I tell her "I'm going to cum" and tighten up my but cheeks.

I grab the back of her neck and let a big fat nut off. Holding her head down with one hand and clinching the chair with the other hand.

She is not stopping and it feels painfully good to nut inside her mouth.

As I sit there, sort of fighting her, trying not to say anything because I didn't want anyone to hear us. She holds all my cum in her mouth and continues sucking until I have to push her away off me. She spits all of my cum into some napkins and looks at me and says "did you like that"?

I tell her whispering, "I don't believe that just happened". She smiles and takes a drink from her soda. I zip my pants back up and look around to see if anyone saw what had just happened. No one is looking and I tell her thank you so much Sexy. You are something else. She says don't mention it. It's my treat to you Good.

I try to watch the rest of the movie in awe that we just had movie sex. Wow, I never had movie sex before so I lean over and whisper into her ear. "I never had movie sex before". She laughs and tells me that she had never done anything like that before either. We finish the movie and the credits start to roll up the screen. I ask her if she is ready to go and she says sure.

We get up and start to leave the theater leaving everything right there and I tell wait. I turn around and pick up the popcorn box and soda to throw away. We walk down the stairs and leave out the theater. I throw away the trash and we go to the bathrooms. She tells me that she will be right back and we both go into the restrooms.

I try to wipe myself up a little bit and wash my hands. I come out of the bathroom and of course she is still inside so I wait for her and then she comes out. We walk out of the movies and to the car. I open the car door for her as I always do and she tells me "Good, you are such a gentleman". She kisses me and gets into the car. I shut the door and walk around to the other side. I get in my ride and we take off.

She asks me if we could go somewhere else, she didn't feel like going home just yet. I tell her sure and I take her to a pool hall. We go inside and go to a table. I get some change and put it into the table.

I tell her to rack em up. She tries to but doesn't have a clue on what ball goes where. So I show her how to arrange the balls with the 8 ball in the middle.

I ask her if she knows how to break and she says no. I tell her to come around here at the front of the table and show her how to hold her stick. We laugh and laugh because she says I never thought that you would be teaching me how to hold a stick.

I scoot behind her really close and show her how to move the stick, aiming for the ball you want to hit. She is having a fun time and we both laugh it up because she doesn't have a clue. We spend a lot of time doing nothing and she screams when a ball finally goes in.

I try not to hit a ball in so she can actually think that she is doing something. So it's now about 1:30 in the morning and I tell her that I have to go. She tells me that she is having a great time and she loves spending time with me.

As we get back to the car and take off, she tells me that she really feels comfortable with me and that she can do anything with me. She doesn't do the things we do together with anyone else. She made me feel really special when she told me that. She says that she is only a freak with me and she is always a lady in the street. I told her that I love her singing and I think that we are going to always be friends for ever. She tells me that she loves my sax and my sex.

I say "hey, that sounds like a song or something". She laughs and gives me a great big smile.

I get her to her place and walk her to the door. She gives me a great big hug and kisses and tells me the she really had a great time tonight. I tell her that I really enjoyed her too.

She says you sure you don't want to come inside. I tell her no, I have to get up in the morning and if I come in she knows what's going to happen. She asks "can you go to work from here". I really want you to come in. so I tell her well no babe. I will see you later. I leave and race home to get me some sleep. I crash out when I get home for it was a very good day.

Chapter Eleven

I wake up the next morning to get ready for work. I head out the door almost late, jump in my ride and get there in minutes flat. Run inside and clock in. Think to myself, man I barley made it. Reminiscing on the night before, I think about Sexy. What a freaky woman. She is too much. I'm gonna have to get in tight with her. She is too kinky and she aint scared either.

I call up Tangy and see how she is doing. Ring, ring, ring, "Hello", I say. "Hello", a sexy voice answers.   "May I speak to Tangy" I ask.

"This is she", she answers.

"Who is calling"?

I tell her that it is Good and she says "Hi" in a very excited voice. "How have you been Tangy", I ask her?

She tells me that she has been pretty good and the she is so sorry about the other day. I tell her that it is ok and don't worry about it. I ask her if she is not busy later maybe we can go out and get something to eat. She says sure she would be delighted to do that. I tell her that I get off at 3 o'clock and she says she will be home around 4 o'clock. I tell her that that's fine and I will see her later. She tells me bye and we hang up the phones.

I go though my day and all I can think about is Tangy. She was so pretty and tall and very classy. I can't wait to see her. At my lunch time I grab something to eat and go out to my car to make some phone calls. First I call Baby to see how she is doing.

"Hello Baby, how are you darling". She answers "fine" and we talk a little bit about how such a great time we had together. I tell her that we have to get together soon and have some more fun.

She ask me if I want to come by her job again and I tell her not today and she says o.k. just let me know and I will make plans for you to come by. I tell her o.k. and she says that she has to go and I tell her that I will talk to her later on tonight. We say our goodbyes and hang up.

Then I call up Denise. Baby's co-worker. The phone rings and Denise answers. "Hello darling" I say in my foreign voice. She says hello bake and I ask her when I can see her. She says that maybe we can get together on the weekend, and goes on to tell me that she is going to be very busy all week. I think that she is trying to put me off so I ask her.

"Are you trying to put me off"? And she tells me No, not at all. It's just that I am very busy with my work this week. I tell her o.k. so I'll talk to you later and have a nice day sweetheart. We say bye and hang up.

I call up sticks and ask him if we are going to rehearse today and he says "yhea man, come by about 6 o'clock". I tell him that I have to go get my axe before I come by. He tells me alright man, so I'll see you after you get off the job.

"Peace out Sticks", I tell him.

"Later, Good", he answers.

After work that day. I head home to grab my axe. As I'm driving down the street I call Sexy to see if she's coming to the rehearsal. She answers her phone and we great each other. I say, "Hey Sexy". "Hey Good, how are you"? She asks. Im good Sexy, always good baby. She says what's up and I ask her if she is coming to the rehearsal and she says oh, o.k. I'll be there in a little while. I tell her o.k. you sexy thing you. I will see you there. We say our goodbyes and we hang up the phones.

I get home and run in to grab my horn. When I get inside my phone rings and I answer it.

"Hello".

I hear a familiar female voice say, "Hi Good, how are you"?

"I'm fine but not as fine as you, I answer. It's Alize right"?

"Yhea, it's me".

"What you doin"? She ask me and I tell her that I'm going to a rehearsal. She goes on to tell me that she really had a great time and hopes that we can get together later on. She tells me that she doesn't know what got into her and that she never acts like that. I tell her not to worry I am not going to disrespect her in any way and I had a great time also. I tell her that maybe we can get together later on this week and she says "fine, I would love that". I'll talk to you later baby, I have to go. I tell her.
She says o.k., you have a good day and we say bye and hang up the phone.

I pick up my sax and head out of the door. Run to the car and get inside. Start up the engine and put it in drive. I pull out into traffic and speed off to meet Tangy for something to eat before rehearsal.

I call up Tangy and ask her if she's ready to go get something to eat. She says sure, I'm starving. I get to her place and call her back to let her know that I'm outside in the front. She tells me that she will be out in a second.

As I'm waiting for Tangy to come out of the building, Sexy walks up and says "Hey Good, what you doin here"?

I tell her that I'm waiting for a friend and she ask me if it was Keys. I tell her no and before she could ask my anymore questions Tangy walks out of the building. And I get out of the car and walk around to open the door for Tangy. I introduce Sexy to Tangy and Sexy says hello with this look on her face like she was jealous or something.

I open the car door and let Tangy into the car and close the door. I look at Sexy as I walk around the car to get in and she is looking at me with her eyes squinted as if she was really angry at me. I don't know why she would be so angry, we are only friends and she is not my girlfriend.

I pull off and tangy ask me who was that? I tell her that she sings in with the band sometimes and she is also a friend that lives in the building. Have you seen her before I ask? She tells me no and that she doesn't really talk to a lot of people in her building. I stay to myself she says.

"So, what do you want to eat"? I ask her. She says "well I don't eat meat. I'm a vegetarian".

"Oh, so were can we get something for you to eat"? I ask her.
She says that there is a little place right around the corner and they are not at all expensive.

So we drive around the corner and she directs me to the place. I pull into the parking lot and park the car. I get out and walk around to open her door and she opens it and says "Good, you don't have to do that for me. It's nice and all, but we just going casual right now. If we were going out to a fancy restaurant all dressed up, then you can open the door for me". I couldn't believe she said that. She was cool as a fan. Beautiful, and really down to earth.

So we go inside and she orders something for herself as I look in confusion. She asks me if I like mushrooms. I tell her yes. She asks me if I like corn and I tell her yes. Then she suggests that I get some vegetable stir fry with oyster sauce. I tell her that sounds delicious. Then I see the lady behind the counter pouring something that looks like cream into a cold beverage. I ask the lady what is that, which she is making. She tells me that it is Ti-Tea and asks me if I want to taste it. I tell her yhea, sure and she pours me a small glass.

I sip it and it is wonderful. "Mmmmmmmm", I say. I then ask Tangy if she has ever had it and she says no. I tell her that she must taste it. She does and likes it. So I tell the woman behind the counter to give us two large Teas please.

So we get our food and sit down right there in the restaurant. I start to enjoy the food as she does also. I tell her that it is very good and I thought that all veggie food was not so tasty. She laughs and tells me that is not true at all. We go on talking about food for awhile and I tell her that food is sexual. She says oh really. I tell her hell yhea it is. Food and sex has been linked together all the way back to the Garden of Eden. She says "wow, you don't say".

We start to talk about vegetables and how vitamins in them play a big part in health and sex life. She is amazed at how much I seem to know about veggies and I can tell that she is impressed with it.

So after we eat and drink the tea. I take her back to her building and get out walking her to her door.

I hold her hand as we walk into the building and she tells me thanks so much for dinner. I tell her I really want to spend more time with her but I have rehearsal tonight.

She says I understand, don't worry. I will be seeing you again. I smile at her and she gives me a smile back. I tell her that I hope her sister doesn't take it too hard and she says that she's got plenty of men. She can afford to loose one good one. I laugh and she say's I'm serious. You seem like you're a good one so far.

We get to her door and I tell her would it be too soon to kiss her and she says no, not at all. We kiss right there at her door and the door opens. It's her sister and she says "I thought I heard someone out here".

Tonya walks away from the door and I tell Tangy that I will definitely see her later to pick up were we left off. She says be careful what you wish for and winks at me and tells me bye. I say bye but I don't let go of her hand. We stand there for a brief moment as if we didn't want to let go of each others hands. Then I let go and walk away.

I get down to the car and jump in and start heading for practice. I arrive at Sticks place and grab my axe and head inside. Sexy is already there and so is Keys. I start setting up and Keys comes over to me and says Hey Good. You know you pissed off Sexy right. I tell him that I know but we are only friends and she will have to except that. She comes over to us and says "You dog, you know you wrong". I look up at her and she goes on and on saying that you fuckin with a bitch in my own building. How could you be so cold? I thought that we were better than that. You aint shit but a dog ass nigga.

Then I look at her and ask her is she finished, can I say something. She says what? What?

I tell her in a smooth calming voice that she is just somewhat of a friend and we just went to get something to eat. That's all. Why are you acting like your in high school? I thought higher of you than this Sexy.

She looks as if she was embarrassed because she told Keys a bunch of shit that wasn't his biz. I tell her that she is still my baby. But you can't be acting like that. I don't deal with jealous ass women and you aint my woman anyway.

She suddenly says she's sorry to me and then apologizes to Keys and Sticks. She says that she let her emotions take control of her. She gives me a great big hug and kisses me on the cheek.

Sticks looks at us both and says you see what happens when you have sex. She tells him to shut up. You were tryin to get at me too. And we all start laughing it up.

Left walks in and says what's so funny? We all look at him and say oh nothing; you had to be there man Sticks says.

We finish setting it up and kick off a nice little groove to warm up to. Quick comes in and Left says "Late as usual".

He sets up his guitar and we start our rehearsal for the new gig. We decide on a song list that we are going to play. And we go down the line. Keys says "so is Sexy on for the show or what"?

I ask Sexy is she willing to do it for free because we didn't include her in the price that we quoted. She says that she will do it for me as a favor. I remind her that if she makes a commitment that she has to honor it no matter what. She says ok. I say "even if you see me fucking someone else".

She says ok, but don't go there.

Quick says, "What the fuck. Where did that come from"? Left says, Aw shit, its some freaky-freaky shit going one here. Sexy tells them both to shut up.

We go on with the rehearsal and we are really sounding good on all the songs. I tell Sexy that she sounds great and she has to make all the rehearsals until the gig. She says o.k.

After practice, we are all joking around and laughing while we put our instruments away. Sexy comes over and says do you want some company tonight Good. I tell her that I'm kinda tired and probably need to get some sleep. She says that tonight is the night. I ask her what does that mean? She asks me if I had any KY gel. And my face lights up.

I tell her to meet me at home. She says ok and we both leave almost simultaneously.

I race home quickly and anxiously. I'm going to get some anal from Sexy. She has that most rounded shapely, softest ass you ever want to see and touch. It looks like a heart upside down. When you say apple bottom, you think of Sexy. If you look up the word "Great Ass" in the dictionary, you would see a picture of hers in there.

I run into my place and light up some candles. I hear a knock on the door. I know it's her so I run to the door and answer it. Yep, it's Sexy.

"Come on in baby". I grab her hand and pull her into my place. She starts up saying how foolish she was earlier and that she was so sorry. I'm thinking to myself, you gone be sorry when I get in that ass.

I ask her if she wants anything to drink and she says no thank you. I lead her into the bed room and start to take my clothes off wasting no time. She starts to undress herself and tells me that the candles are very nice. We both stand there half dressed and I walk toward her. She takes my hand and puts it on her breast. We start to kiss and caress each other.

I back her up to the bed and push her down on the bed. I jump on top of her and start to kiss her lips. Then I kiss her ear, sucking the ear lobe. Then I move down to the neck and she loves it. She is starting to moan and groan already.

I put one of the twins into my mouth and start licking the nipple. Then I suck it slowly as I squeeze it at the same time. I touch her vagina and yes it is wet and ready but I know just what I want from her.

I ask her for the KY gel. She says let me get it out of my purse. She goes and gets her purse and pulls out some KY gel. I pull off all my clothes and tell her to get naked. She pulls off the rest of her clothes and tells me to let her guide it in and that she has never done it before.
I tell her "o.k., just take your time Sexy and relax".

I can tell that she is not relaxed because she is tensing up. I tell her to get into the doggy style position and she does. I ask her to put some KY on my thumb so I can play with her ass with my thumb first. She puts some on my thumb and I rub my thumb on her ass hole. She moans and tells me to be gentle. I tell her to let me know if it doesn't feel good. She says alright, she will.

I poke her hole with just the tip of my thumb and she loves it. Yhea, daddy she says. I stick my thumb all the way inside her ass and she tells me "ooh yhea baby, I like it".

I tell her that I'm ready. And ask her "are you ready"? She says "Yes". She grabs the KY gel and puts some on my penis witch is extremely hard and erect now. She holds my dick and guides it in slowly.

First, just the head. She moans oooohhhh. Then she pulls it out and puts it back in, but just the head.

"Oooooohhhh, baby. That feels good". Then she pulls it out and puts it back in a little more and more every time she puts it back into her tight little hole until she is relaxed and it's almost all the way in.

She moans every time I go inside of her. Louder and louder she gets as I get deeper and deeper. Now she is relaxed and I'm deep inside of her. I start to thrust slowly and she begs for more and more. Louder and louder she gets.

I tell her to grab a pillow and put her face into it so it doesn't sound like I killing her to my neighbors. Every stroke she screams oh, yhea, ooh, yes, aww, shit, yhea, ooh, oh, yes….

With her head still in the pillow, I slap her on the ass to make her loosen up. She screams with passion.

"Good, Good, Gooooood" she screams as I pound her tight little ass hole. She says "I'm Cuming, I'm cuuuummmiiiinnngggg".

I continue to pound her tight little hole and I can't take any more because the hole is so tight. I pull out and cum all over her ass while rubbing it in with my penis as if it was lotion. She moans and groans even after I pull out and I ask her if she is alright. She says oh yes daddy. I'm good.

I stagger to the bathroom and turn on some hot water. Grab a towel and wet it. I wipe myself and get a towel for her. I wet the towel and bring it to her. She takes the towel and tells me "Wow, I don't believe that I came from that". I tell her me either.

I lie on the bed beside her and lean over to give her a kiss and say thanks baby. She kisses me back and says don't mention it. She says to me "this towel is not going to do it baby. I need to get into the shower".

I tell her to go right ahead; I'm just going to lay here for a minute. As she takes a shower I fall asleep. She wakes me when she's dressed and tells me to let her out. I get up and wipe my face. Stagger over to the door and give her a kiss goodbye. She tells me Goodnight and walks away. I watch her walk for a second or two then I shut the door and go back to lie down. Before I fall into a deep sleep, I stare at the ceiling and think that she did this out of spite because she saw Tangy with me.

I call up Tangy just to say Goodnight. The phone rings and she answers it. "Hello".

"Hello Tangy, it's Good".

She says "Hi Good, how are you"?
I tell her "I'm fine but I was thinking about you and just wanted to say goodnight before I fell asleep".

She says "Oh how sweet. Goodnight sweetheart".

I tell her that I will call her tomorrow and to have a goodnight. She says ok and we hang up the phones. I then have a bigger, greater smile on my face and I fall into a deep sleep.

As I sleep in start having a very strange dream. I'm dreaming of three ladies chasing me with knives and one has a gun. I run away from them but I can never get to far away. They always seem to know where I am and start chasing me again. Trying to cut me and the one with the gun points it at me but I run away before she can shoot it. I fall down and they almost catch me but I get back up and run away. The strange thing about this dream is that they are in sexy night wear. And one of the ladies had a vibrator one time pointing it at me as if it was a weapon. Then the dream goes a way.

When I wake up in the morning I feel like a new man. One who has conquered a great thing? I have made Sexy give in to me that plump brown round ass. It really isn't a great big deal, but this doesn't happen everyday because a lot of women think that it is very painful and that no way can you get an orgasm from it. I say "You better ask somebody". I got one and so did my partner.

Chapter Twelve

On the way to work I stop to get some coffee. Not too much sugar and a lot of cream. I make some phone calls to start off the day. First I call up Tangy.

"Hello Tangy, how are you"?

"Hi Good, I'm fine. How are you sweetheart"?

I answer, "I'm much better now beautiful". And she laughs.

I tell her that I would love to see her again and she says me too and that she really enjoyed our time together. I ask her if she is going to be free after I get off work about four o'clock and she says sure. "Just give me a call and I would love to see you again".

I tell her that I think that she is a very beautiful person and that I will see her later on tonight. Have a great day sweetheart. She tells me also to have a great day and we both hang up our phones.

I then call up Baby.

"Hello Darling, how var you"? I ask her in my foreign voice.

She says, I'm fine darling. How are you? I tell her that I miss her very much and I can't live without her. She laughs and says "Good, you are so crazy". I start singing, "Baby, I need your good lovin. Got, to have all your sweet lovin".

She laughs some more and tells me just call me and we will get together. I tell her that I will call her later and have a nice day. She says bye and we both hang up.

I call up Denise and she picks up.

"Hello Darling, how var you"? In my foreign voice.

She says "I'm good Mr. Good. How are you this morning"?

I tell her that I'm much better now. And she laughs also. I ask her when we are going to get to see each other. And she says "How about Friday. Is Friday good for you"?

I tell her that Friday is good but I do have a rehearsal on the day. It would have to be later on in the evening. She says "Ok, that's fine. That gives me some time to get myself together after work". I tell her "So Friday it is. I can't wait to see you again and have a great day today beautiful". She says by Mr. Good and we hang up our phones.

I arrive at work and clock in. I get to my desk and see Chris. "Hey Chris what's good man". He tells me just chillin man. "You know man, another day, another dollar". I answer; "You know that's right man.

I ask him how that situation with his ex turned out. He tells me that everything is cool now that he let her give him some more of that bomb head. I tell him "Say what"!

"Yhea man, after all that drama here. I had to call her and tell her that she can't come up here to the job no more and that she better not be acting like a crazy bitch any more. She knows that I have a lady now and I am not giving her up. So she is just going to have to deal with it or leave me alone".

"She told me that as long as I don't throw it in her face we can be good friends. So I went over there and got some more of that brain. Man, she opens the door for me and I go inside. She has the candles going and some food in the oven. She tells me how sorry she is and let her make it up to me".

"So I sit on the couch and she comes over and gets on her knees. Unbuckles my pants and unzips me". "She starts pulling and sucking on my dick so I pull off my pants and she goes on telling me "baby I'm so sorry. You know that I will do anything for you".

"I kick back and put my hands on the top of my head as she slurps and gobbles my dick. She starts that humming thing and I tell her "Mmmmmm, it feels so good".

"She cups my balls and holds them as she sucks me and then she starts stroking me with her other hand. I couldn't take anymore so I tell her that I'm going to cum and she lets me cum in her mouth and kept on sucking".

"She swallowed all of my cum and listened to me as I begged her to stop".

"I curled up like a little baby and then she went to the bathroom and got a warm rag to wipe me off. Man, that was some great head she gave me Good.

"My girl don't ever do it like that for me man".

I tell him that yhea, but you with your girl for a reason. She must make you happier than Crissy.

"Man, Crissy is crazy and she can't be trusted dog. I tell him, "You see".

He says, "She sure got some good head though". We both laugh and he walks away.

He stops and turns around and says "Oh, there's a BBQ on Sunday at the park man. The Riders are giving it and everything is free. Free BBQ, free beer, free bitch's". We both laugh and he walks away from my desk.

I sit there and start back at my work. At around ten thirty I give Sticks a call.

"Yo, Sticks. What's up man"?

"What's up with you Good, what it do?" he answers.

I tell him I hear there's going to be a BBQ at the park on Sunday. Oh yhea! He answers.

"Yhea man, we gotta get us some BBQ. You know that Big Daddy is going to cook it up. He always brings his giant BBQ trailer and smokes up the whole city".

We laugh and Sticks says "man, last time I ate his BBQ, it was so good I bit one of my fingers". We laugh some more. He tells me "Yhea, that cat is down by law". He pauses and says "Good, you know Sexy really likes you man. I think she wants to have your baby". We both start cracking up. I tell him "You crazy man, I aint havin noooo kids for nobody.

"I'll get at you later Sticks. I gotta go". Sticks says "Alright peace out daddy-o". We both hang up our phones.

Later at lunch time I call up Baby to see how she is. The phone rings. Baby picks up.

"Hey Baby, how you doin"?

She says, "I'm doing fine Good. What's up"?

"Oh, I just wanted to hear your voice and smell your perfume through the phone". She says "You know you can't smell my perfume through the phone Good".

I tell her that I can imagine how it smelled that last time I saw her. Then I ask her if I could see her soon.

"I really need to see you baby". She says maybe on the week end. I am really busy this week and I have to finish some assignments'. I tell her ok, that's not a problem, and I don't want to interrupt your busy work schedule.

I then tell her that if she has a free moment to call me and let me know so we can get together. She tells me ok and that she wants to see me again also. It's just that she is a little busy this week. I tell her ok so just give me a call and we can get together. She tells me that maybe I can come by her job for lunch again if I know what she means. I said anytime baby. Just let me know and I'm there. She says how about tomorrow? I tell her ok, sure. Tomorrow I am there, around twelve noon right. She agrees, yes twelve noon daddy. I tell her that I can't wait to see her and she says me too. I tell her bye and to have a nice day. She says you do the same. Bye bye. We hang up our phones.

I go on with the rest of my day as usual and I get a phone call almost before I get off. It's Alize. I answer the phone in my foreign voice.

"Hello darling, how var you"?

She answers "I'm just fine Good. How are you"?

I tell her that I'm always good. What's going on with you?

She tells me that she was wondering if I wanted to see her today. I tell her sure baby. I always want to see you. Then she asks me if I could pick her up from the beauty shop? I tell her that I get off in ten minutes. "Are you ready right now"?

She says that they will be done in about an hour. I tell her great I will come there after I get off work. So what is the address to the beauty shop? She tells me it's on the corner of El Segundo and Van Ness right behind the Kentucky Fried Chicken. I tell her that I know exactly where she is. I've been there before and I know the owner through a friend.

She says ok, so I will see you later then. I answer; "Goodbye Love" and we both hang up.

I get off work and I run by Tangy's place to see how she is doing. I run inside and ring her door. There's no answer so I call her up. Ring, ring, she answers. "Hello".

"Hey Tangy, It's Good".

She says "Hey Good, how are you"?

"I'm so sorry I had to come to the shop. They said that they could squeeze me in today so I rand down here. You can see me later after I'm all prettied up if you like".

I tell her "Sure, I would love to see you, but it's hard for me to imagine that you could be even prettier than you already are". She say's "Aaaawwww, You are so sweet".

"So I will see you later ok".

I tell her "Ok beautiful", and we hang up.

Now, how was I to know that the same beauty shop that she was at, was the same shop that Alize was sitting in at the same moment?

I leave Tangy's place and start for the beauty shop. I arrive to the beauty shop and I park in the parking lot. I phone Alize to see if she is ready yet. The phone rings.

"Hello", she says.

"Hi, are you ready yet"? I ask her. She says "No not yet. It's going to be just a few minutes still. You can come inside if you want too".

I tell her "Ok, I'll be inside in a few minutes I have to make a call".

So as I'm sitting out in the parking lot, I start to think. I wonder if Tangy is in the same shop. This could be an awkward moment if I go inside and there both inside the same shop. So I sit there and wait for a moment.

I get a phone call and it's Tangy on the phone. I answer the phone and she says to me.

"Are you stalking me? I see you out in the parking lot". I tell her you do? She says yhea, I'm paying my bill I will be right out. I tell her ok. And we hang up.

I think to myself, Oh shit! What the hell am I going to do? Then I see Tangy coming out of the beauty shop and she is gorgeous. I forgot all about Alize and got out of the car walked up to Tangy and said you are really a beautiful lady. She smiles at me and I tell her that her carriage is waiting.

I open the door for her and I start to walk around the car and I see Alize paying for her stuff at the register. I open the door and give Tangy the keys and tell her that I have to go inside and tell the owner hello. I haven't seen him a few years.

I run inside and tell Alize that I'm sorry something came up and I have to leave without her. She says hold on, she is finished and she will be coming out right now. I tell her that there has been an emergency and I have to go right now. I turn for the door and she tells me you can't wait a minute, I will be right there. I tell her that I will explain later and I have to go.

I run out of the beauty shop and she comes out not long after me. I'm in the car and I start the engine. I put it in drive and start to pull off. I head for the exit and just as I'm leaving I see Alize looking at my car. I'm thinking Oh shit! I know she saw me and Tangy. Tangy calls my name "Good"?

I answer, Yhea baby. She says why did we leave out of the parking lot so fast and who was that girl looking in the car at us. I tell her "Tangy. I'm going to be totally honest with you. That was my friend that I was supposed to pick up and take home. But I saw you and had a change of plans". She answers "Good, you so crazy".

"Now who was that"? She asks me again.

I answer. "I told you. That was a friend that I was supposed to pick up and take her home but I saw you and had a change of plans".

Then the phone rings. I look at it and its Alize. I look at Tangy and tell her I don't want to take this call, it's her and I cancel the call. She looks at me and says I sure hope you know what you're doing, because I sure don't.

I look at her and say you're not mad. She says no, what should I be mad for. I'm in the car and she's the one that doesn't have a ride. I start laughing and say to her, you know Tangy, you are really cool people. Then she looks at me and says "It's not like were having sex or anything". And my face drops because she is right. I have not had sex with her yet. Man, did I feel bad.

I left Alize right there in the parking lot and drove off with Tangy and we had sex before and it was really good. I felt like I had dogged her out. I then call her back while Tangy was in the car and tell her that I'm sorry I will be right back to pick her up. I have to drop someone off and then I hang up the phone. Tangy says, do whatever you gotta do.

"Are you coming back by"? I tell her yes, after I drop her off. I will come back bye.

So I take Tangy home and tell her that I will see her later and she gives me a kiss on the lips and says "you better just be giving her a ride home".

I tell her "I am, don't worry. I have my eyes locked on you baby". She tells me that she will see me later and I drive off.

I call up Alize and tell her that I'm on my way and she says I am so mad at you. You better get here fast as you can. I tell her I'll be there in less than ten minutes and hang up.

When I get to the beauty shop I don't see her in the parking lot so I pull up to the door and park. I call up Alize and she answers. "Hello" she says.

I say, "Hey baby were are you"? She says "I'm inside were you at"?

"I'm out in the parking lot" I answer.

She says "I'll be ready in a few more minutes. I had to do something. You can come inside if you like".

I tell her "ok".

So I get out of the car and walk inside the shop. As I enter inside the shop I can feel all eyes on me. I walk over to register were my boy is and say hey Fred, what's up dog, long time no see. He looks at me and says "Good"!

"What's happening man; it's you that's got all the females panties in a bunch."

I tell him "say what".

He goes on and says "Man, they were all in here seconds before you walked in talking about yo ass like you were a dog man". One of the ladies sitting in a chair says "Yhea, you aint shit and we said it".

I tell her wait a minute and she goes on to say   "That's what's wrong with men today. They think that they can just treat women like anything they want". "They don't respect us. They don't love us. And they sure can't protect us. Men today aint shit. Me and Fred are hysterical. She gets even more angry and starts in even more.

"Yall aint good for nothing but some dick. And most of you can't even get that right. Broke ass, weed smoking, beer drinkin, breath stankin dogs".

Tangy walks out from the back and hears all this going on and stops in her tracks puts her hands on her hips and listens. The lady goes on and on.

"Sorry ass, Punk ass, bitch's". I tell Tangy to come on baby lets get the hell out of here. She laughs and says "She's right. You tell em Sha Sha".

I look at Tangy and shake my head and start heading for the door. She knows if she doesn't come on right now that I was going to leave her ass for agreeing with that crazy ass hoe. And if she didn't know that, she was about to find out.

I open the car and get in. put the key into the ignition and I see Tangy coming out of the shop. I lean over and open the door for her and she gets in. I start the car up and drive off.

She looks at me and says "Ok Good. What the hell was that all about earlier? You got some other bitch in your car and you were supposed to pick me up. What the hell is wrong with you? You better have a good one for me". Then she just looks at me.

I start off "Tangy, I am not going to lie to you. That was my friend and she needed a ride home. You weren't ready so I figured that I could take her home and come right back and get you". She says "You a damn lie, you saw me paying for my shit and you left me.

You must be fucking that bitch". I tell her "No, I swear to God I am not fucking her. We have never had sex before. I put that on everything I love". She looks at me and says you know I can tell when someone is lying and something seems kinda funny.

"You seem to be telling me the truth though but I don't know. Something just doesn't seem right".

"You sure you aren't fucking her? I tell her "I'm sure, baby. I am not fucking her" and I think to myself (Yet).

She says so what's up then. I just think that we jump the gun a little bit and now my emotions are all involved. I tell her that she don't have to worry, I would never hurt her on purpose. I tell her to lean over and give me a kiss. So she does. I ask her were exactly does she live and how to get there. She tells me the address and starts on the directions.

I get to her place and she asks me if I want to come inside for a little while. I think about Tangy and tell her sure but I have to go take care of some business. She says yhea right. You know you going to see that bitch probably. I tell her "no, not at all. I will come back after I take care of my business. If that's all right, that is".

She says what ever and gets out of the car as walks away mad. I leave and go back to see Tangy.

Chapter Thirteen

When I get to Tangy's place and call her up to tell her that I'm outside and she tells me to hold on she will let me in shortly. She comes to open the door and we walk inside.

She says to me, "I know she cursed you out".

I ask her "why do you say that".

She answers, "Because I would have been pissed off if you came to get me and I see you drive off with another bitch".

I tell her "You know your right".

"That was pretty fucked up and I shouldn't have done it". "But I am a little crazy about you and I think I want you to be my number one".

She looks at me and says "Your number one, you mean your one and only". I tell her that when I'm with her, I don't think of no one else and she makes me so happy. We have good times together.

She says back to me, "Only time will tell". So I go inside her place and I ask her "Where is your sister"?

"I know that she don't like me or even want to see me in here.

She says that she is gone and should not be back for another five hours.

"So relax and don't worry about it. I took care of her when I had to get her straight. She was going to play you like a flute and just try to get money out of you. She has so many guys calling here all times of the day and night. She even has a sex line where they call and she goes into the room to talk dirty to them and tells them there fantasies.

I thought wow, I'm glad I didn't get involved with her. I look at Tangy and tell her thank you. She says for what? I tell her "Thank you for saying what you said when you first saw me". If you didn't say "Does the cat have any more out there like him", I would still probably be chasing your sister".

Even when I first saw you, I knew that you were so beautiful and I was really amazed at your smile. I wasn't thinking about your sister after I saw you. And it's funny how it just fell in to place. And I didn't have to make a fool out of myself by trying to talk to two sisters at the same time.

"Thank you". I grab her hand. Look her in her eyes and tell her "I will always be there for you. I want you for my lady".

She smiles back at me and kisses me on the lips. I kiss her back and grab her and pull her closer to me. Kissing her passionately, I feel her up and she says "Yes, I want you too. Take me I'm yours".

I back her up to the wall and we start undressing each other. I unbutton her shirt. She unbuckles my pants. Off goes my shirt and she takes hers off too. I kiss her on the neck and unbutton her bra. I take one of her breast and grab it. I start licking on the nipple and around her areola. I put the whole areola in my mouth and suck it gently while licking the nipple and then gently biting the tip softly.

She moans and I suck a little harder and faster. I moan and tell her that she taste so good. She says "That feels so good" in a soft whispering voice. I grab the other breast and start on that one. Sucking the nipple slowly and then licking it. Sucking the areola and then licking around it, gently biting on the nipple. She tells me "Ooooh that feels so good".

I walk her into the bedroom and ask her to take off her pants. We take all of our clothes off and stand there naked looking at each other. I back her over to the bed and push her down on the bed briskly. I climb on top of her slowly and kiss her in the mouth. My tongue slowly licks around her lips and she loves it. I taste her tongue with my tongue and we both start to feel the heat rise getting a little warmer.

I kiss her neck and she moans. I touch her soft hairy pussy and it is wet and warm. I search for the clit in her wetness and find it between her slippery soft fleshy parts. She gasp's as I touch her clit and rub on it slowly.

"Yes Good, that feels so good" she tells me.

I kiss her breast slowly and tickle her nipples for a moment as I continue to go down farther on her body exploring her soft tender skin. I get to the navel and I lick around it and then kiss it. She moans some more and tells me "You are driving me crazy".

I kiss her around her warm womb and spread her thighs and then kiss her on the inner thigh. Then I move to the other inner thigh and kiss it too.

I suck on her thigh as to give her a monkey bite on the inside of her thigh and she moans "Oooooohhhhh, that's right".

I then move up to the wet, fleshy, warm pussy. I start to lick it slowly around searching for the clit. I spread apart her vagina lips as if I was looking for her hot pink insides. I lick and then suck on her clit. She moans and groans for more.

"Yes, baby". "That feels so good baby". She says to me.

I love the wetness of her slippery warm pussy. I start to tease her by sticking my tongue inside her but just a little bit. It seems to drive her wild. And then I lick up and down her lips and back to the clit. Sucking her clit slowly at first and then a little faster. She is starting to get a little louder as she tells me those yes sounds.

"Yes, baby".

"Yes baby". "Ooooohhhhh shit". She cries.

I ask her if she likes it and she agrees.

"Yes baby I like it. I like it".

I ask her is she going to cum and she says almost. So I keep on sucking and licking her sweet sugar walls. She grabs my head and pulls on my ears. That is a signal that she may be Cuming. So I go in for the kill. I suck the clit very strong and lick it very fast. Changing from suck to lick and she is going crazy moaning and groaning and then all of the sudden she start screaming out very loud.

"Oh! Yes! Oh! Yes! Good! Yes Good"!

I am surprised at this because I have never had a screamer before. She is really loud and I know that everyone around can hear her. This made my dick very hard and I wanted her even more now.

I start to slow down a little and she calms down and gets quieter. I ask her if she is ready for daddy. She says "Oh yes baby". "Give it to me".

I grab a condom out of my pants and open it up. Slide it on and pull her over to the edge of the bed. Lean over her and kiss her on the lips ever so gently and slide the head of my dick onto her. She sighs and says "Oh, yes daddy. More".

I slide my dick all the way inside of her and she moans and grabs me. "Oooohhhh, Yes baby".

"Get it daddy, Get it", she tells me.

I start to stoke her just little faster and more and more hard. The pussy is so good I know that I can't last for ever. So I stop stoking after about ten humps and start over again.

Pushing it all the way in as I stop each time. She loves it, as I stop she moans "Oooohhhh yhea baby".

I tell her to turn over so I can hit it from behind doggy style. She jumps right up to it. Gets on her hands and knees and looks at me from behind. I slide inside her and she tells me to ride it baby. I slide all the way inside her and she moans "That's right, give it to me".

I tell her this is some good pussy. She tells me to get it daddy. I slap her on the ass as I stroke her just a little faster and harder. She starts telling me that she is going to cum again and now I can't take all this nasty talk and start to rise to my climax.

My dick is getting really extremely hard and I start to pound on the pussy, stroking in and out furiously, as if I was trying to hurt her wet pussy. Pounding all the way in and pulling back out. Pounding some more all the way in and pulling out. With every stroke, she starts to cum again.

"Yhea baby", she cries out louder and louder.

"Oh yhea daddy". "Yes. Yes".

I start slapping her on her ass as she cums for me. "Oh, Good. Oh, Good".

I tell her "I'm going to cum baby, I'm going to Cuuummmm", and then I cum for her too. I give her a couple of last mercy humps and she gives me a few last Yes sounds.

There I lay behind her as my body slumps over her like I ran out of gas but still holding her ass. She asks me if I'm alright and I tell her yes baby, I'm alright. I start to pull out slowly and we both give each other our last ooohhh's.

I collapse on the bed and she starts to caress me. She tells me that was so good baby. I agree with her. Yhea baby, that was really good.

She gets up and goes to the bathroom and I hear the water run. She comes back out with a warm rag and tells me, "Here, let me wipe you off and clean you up a little bit".

She pulls the rubber off gently as my penis is still hard but very sensitive and I give her an "oooh baby".

She asks me if it is sensitive and I tell her yhea baby. She wipes my penis and balls off and then throws the rubber away. I lay there as if I was in heaven staring at the ceiling. She comes back and lies beside me and we hold each other for a little while talking and giggling about really nothing.

I tell her that I want her to be my lady and she says that I would have to make up my mind about that. I ask her what does she mean and she tells me that she knows that I have friends because of what happened today. So I would have to make up my mind if that is what I really want.

She goes on to tell me that she will not be second or even first. She has to be the one and only in my life.

I tell her that I understand exactly what she is saying and that I have a lot of female friends so it may take some time. She says I do have brothers and I know that if you are not ready to make a commitment then it will not work. You have to make up your mind she says.

I lay there and think about her and wonder if she is the one for me. Do I want to spend the rest of my life with this woman? Or do I just want to have great sex with her like we just had?

I look at her and tell her "Tangy, we are going to have to take it one day at a time".

"I do really like you a lot and I want you to be my lady so I am going to try to be the best man I can be".

She looks at me and says "Don't promise me something that you can't deliver. I need a strong minded man in my life that knows what he wants".

I tell her as I sit up on the bed. "I know what I want and it is you, but I really want to get to know you a lot better before we make any real decisions". She looks at me and says that well maybe we did jump the gun here, but I knew what I wanted and I acted on it.

I felt like I had just got played but didn't mind one bit.

I tell her so you don't have a boyfriend or anything like that do you? She looks at me and says "No, just you Good". I tell her that I have to be honest to her because I do like her very much. I have some friends with benefits. She laughs and says "Its ok I know you do".

"I'm glad you didn't try to lie about it because I would have told you to forget about me".

"It was something about you Good when I first talked to you. You seem to be honest with me about everything we talked about. I admire that in you. Most guys lie to try and kick it with me. You don't have to lie to kick it".

That's when I felt like we were going to be friends for a long time. There was nothing fake about our friendship. She understood me as a man and I understood her as a good woman. She knew that she couldn't change me and I had to change on my own if I wanted her bad enough. So I tried to change from that moment on.

I got up and started to get dressed. She says to me "you have some unfinished business to settle". I tell her yes as if she already knew. I tell her that I will call her later and she says ok.

She walks over to the door and opens it. She watches me walk over towards her as she stands at the door looking very sexy in a short robe. I get to the door and she leans over to kiss me so I kiss her. While I'm kissing her I'm thinking what a lucky guy I am to have a lady in my life like this. I tell her you sure make it easy for me to fall in love with you. She smiles at me and says get out of here Good. I walk out and head for my car.

I get in and call up Alize. Ring, ring, she answers "Hello".

"Hi Alize, how are you" I ask her. She replies, "I'm the same as when you left earlier". I tell her that I'm on my way back and she says all right let me know when you get here so I can let you in. I tell her ok, I'll see you in a minute and hang up.

When I get to Alize's place, I call her to let me in and she comes out and opens the gate for me. She tells me to park in her stall, so I park and we walk inside to her place.

She doesn't say very much to me so I can tell that she is still mad with me. She opens the door and I walk in behind her then she closes the door and stands there. I ask her is she still mad and she says what do you think.

She starts going on and on about how men aren't shit and they always trying to play games. She goes into the kitchen and gets a knife comes back into the front room and ask me if I love the bitch. I look at her and say "what". She walks up closer to me and asks me if I love that bitch. I tell her "No, she is just a friend".

She gives me a really crazy look and points the knife at me and says to me "Don't lie to me. Do you love that bitch".

I look at her as if she wants to play with a knife, she better get ready to get stabbed back with one. She points the knife at my stomach and asks me again do I love that bitch. I walk up to her and tell her no baby I don't love her we are just friends.

Then I grab the knife from her and throw it. I ask her what the fuck, are you crazy or something. I flinch at her as if I was going to knock the holly shit out of her and tell her "Don't you ever in your life pull another knife out on me".

"I will beat the shit out of you girl".

She starts crying saying to me, "I wasn't going to cut you".

"I just wanted the truth from you".

"I wasn't going to cut you".

I grab her by the throat and tell her "You must have lost yo rabbit ass mind".

"Don't you ever pull no shit like that again". She's crying now and says "I'm sorry, I'm sorry".

"I just really like you and I don't want to be played".

I tell her that its ok, I know you were hurt and I'm sorry too baby. I hold her by her waist and kiss her and she kisses me back. We fall into a deep passionate kiss and she tells me to let her make it up to me.

She grabs my hand and walks me into the bedroom. She sits me down on the bed and tells me to take my clothes off as she undresses. All I can think about is Tangy and what I told her. But Alize is so fine.

She takes her shirt off and those breasts are so pretty I start to get a hard on just thinking about sucking them.

She takes off her pants and I start to come out of my pants. She says to me "I want to play that game again Good".

I say to her "Cum for me boo"?

She says "Yes, that's the game".

So we both get undressed and there we are starring at each other naked. She comes over to me and we start to kiss each other. I ask her so who is going to be first? She tells me that I can be first if I want to. I tell her that she is first. Ladies are always first.

She backs onto the bed and sits down. I push her back and tell her to scoot up on the bed. We lie beside each other and kiss some more. She's holding me and I'm holding her as we kiss. Her lips are getting more wet and sweet with each kiss. Her lips are getting softer and softer with each kiss. I hold her close and start to kiss her on the neck and tickle her neck with my tongue. She loves it as I can hear her moan softly.

"Mmmmmm that feels good" she whispers in my ear. I start to go for the breast and lick one of her nipples just to tease her. Then I lick the other as well. Then I go to the other one and put it my mouth. Then I gently suck on both those beautiful twins.

They taste so sweet and tender I get even a harder erection. I grind on her leg as to let her know that I have a hard on for her and I want her badly. I touch her between her legs to see if she is wet and she is.

As I touch her she gives me a sigh. "Oh, yes that feels good".

I start to gently rub her wetness and tell her "Cum for me boo".

I slide my finger up and down her lips but I don't put it inside of her just yet. I touch the opening of her pussy and she tells me "ooh, yes". I slide my finger up and down some more and play with the opening of her pussy. She is getting so excited and I want her even more. I tell her to cum for me boo. I then stick my finger inside of her half way. She tells me "Yes that feels good".

I start to suck on her twins some more and she moans and grinds my finger. I put two fingers inside her and she loves it. I tell her "Cum for me boo". She says "Yes daddy".

I get closer to her and press my body close to hers so she can feel my body heat. She starts gabbing me and squirming. Grinding and giving me all those yes sounds.

I tell her "cum for me boo". She starts breathing heavy and I play with her ass hole a little bit with my pinky finger. She tells me that she is going to cum. I tell her "cum for me boo, cum for me boo".

She grabs me and holds me tightly and she starts to quiver. Suddenly stopping all her movements, she freezes. Then she calls out "Good". I tell her to cum for me boo and she yells out "Oooohhh, yes daddy. I'm Cuming".

I answer, "Cum on baby, cum for daddy". She cums all over my two fingers and it is so slippery wet. She tells me yes daddy, oooohhh, mmmmmm. Yes daddy.

She then turns me over and gets on top of me. Grabs my penis and puts it inside of her. She starts to ride me and grind me. My dick is so hard that she loves it and I tell her you did that baby. It's hard like that because of you.

She grinds me some more and I try to hump her from the bottom of her. Holding her ass cheeks up with both hands and stroking her from under. We both exchange yes sounds and she leans over to kiss me some more.

She puts one of the twins in my mouth and I try to suck it as we fuck at the same time. She looks back and uses one of her hands to stabilize herself. Then she readjusts her legs and starts to fuck me wildly.

Banging her ass down at me we begin to talk to each other almost in tongue.

"Yes baby", "Yes daddy".

"Get it daddy", "Get it baby".

She says "Cum for me boo" as she whips it on me. I start to hump back harder and harder. I say yhea with every hump. She tells me "Uh yhea back with every stride. She say's "cum for me boo". And I tell her "It's Cuuummmmming".

She strokes me some more as I clinch up and give her a few last mercy humps. We exchange our last few moans and Yes sounds and she tells me that's right, give it all to me daddy. Even though the sex was very good, I still was thinking about Tangy. There was something about Tangy that I could not get off my mind or stop thinking about. I go to the bathroom and wash up, get myself together and leave Alize's place. When I get home, I get ready for bed and all I do is think about Tangy. A few minutes pass by and I finally fall asleep.

Chapter Fourteen

The next morning, I wake up and start my day with a cup of coffee. It's a beautiful day outside. The sun is shining and there aren't very many clouds in the sky.

As I head for work I stop to get me a ham and cheese on a bagel. Just before I walk up to the counter to order, I notice a very thick chick looking at me with a smile on her face. I order my bagel and she walks up to me and says "Excuse me, but my name is Red".

"Do you know how to get to the Post Office?"

I tell her "Sure, one second".

I pay for my bagel and get my change. I turn to her and tell her to go about three lights down north and then your going to make a right and go down for about a mile and it will be on the left hand side.

She says "After I make the right turn, I go down were" and looks at my pants zipper.

I smile at her because it is obvious that she needs some attention. She tells me "please can you show me how to get down there".

"I'm not from around here and I'm having a hard time lately". I tell that it is very easy to get to and she won't get lost, but she begins to beg me.

"Please, what did you say your name was"?

I tell her "Good",

"My name is Good". She goes on, "Please show me how to get there".

"I would be so grateful".

"I would do anything if you showed me".

I tell her "I'm sorry but I really don't have the time to show you right now".

She says "Well can we be friends and you can show me later because I don't know a lot about this place and I could use a good friend".

So I tell her "Look you can give me your number but I won't guarantee that I will call you. O.K".

She says o.k. and writes her number down and hands it to me. As I walk away from her she says make sure you call me Good. I could use a good man to show me around". I tell her bye and walk out of the coffee shop. I get in my car and think to myself. Man, old girl was on my dick. That's some easy pussy for sure. I drive off and soon get to work.

At work, it is a regular day for me. On my lunch break, I called Tangy, Baby and Lil Mama. Lil Mama was clownin me about Alize. She says "That bitch aint got shit on me and you know it".

"You know she don't got it like I do". I agree with her because it's true, she is off the chain. Alize got some good sex, but Lil Mama will do what ever I tell her too. And even without a blink of an eye. The more freakier, the more she loves it.

I remember one time she had a lil female friend with her and she tells me to come and get in the bed between both of them. So of course I climb in bed with them and she tells her friend to suck my dick. So she starts sucking and Lil Mama starts to finger fuck her. Her friend is moaning and she is just banging her with her finger. Then she uses two fingers. Then three fingers and before you know it. She is putting all her fingers inside of her pussy.

Then she whips out some KY Gel and squirts some on her hand and slowly pushes her whole hand inside of her pussy. It took a little bit of time to do it, but she did it. And man did that make my dick hard.

She was fisting the girl and she was loving it. Then she asks me what do I want to do to her as if she was getting initiated or something. I tell her nothing and she says back to me "You a damn lie".

She then asks me if I want to fuck her in the ass. And before I could get anything out she jumps up and turns her friend around pointing her ass at me. Spreading her but cheeks apart and tells me to look at that tight lil asshole. Slaps her on the ass and grabs a rubber from the night stand. Throws the rubber at me and says come and get it daddy. I slide the rubber on and she squirts some KY on my dick. I slide the head in and she gasps for air.

"Oooohh", she moans. I slide the head in and out a few more times then Lil Mama slaps me on my ass and tells me to ride that ass daddy.

Lil Mama grabs her titties and starts to suck them. Then she tells me to fuck her harder and harder. Lil Mama's friend loves it. She is groaning and moaning. Telling me "Yes, ooohhh, yes".

Lil Mama starts telling her to tell me to fuck her.

"Say fuck me". She says "Fuck me".

She tells her again "say fuck me". She says "Fuck me". "Oooohhhh". "Fuck me".

I am pounding her tight little ass and tell Lil Mama that I am going to cum. She tells me to pull out. So I pull out and she snatches the rubber off my dick and they both start to lick and jack me off and the same time. This turned me on so much that I almost instantly bust my nut. I squirted nut in Lil Mama's face and then her friend grabbed my dick and I squirted the rest in her face too.

They rubbed my cum in there face with my dick and licked each others face. I was thinking to myself "these bitches are some nasty hoes".

Then I pushed away from them and after they licked all the cum off each others face they came at me for some more. They start licking my balls and Lil Mama tried to lick my ass and I told her "Aw, Hell no".

She said she was sorry and started to lick my dick really slow. It felt so good the two of them licking my balls and dick. I got an instant erection as if it never went down. Lil Mama told her friend "You see, I told you he always stays hard".

Her friend says "Damn Good". I tell them that it's them that makes me so hard, not me.

"Y'all bitches got some real talent". They both laugh at me.

Later that day after work, I head over to Sticks place for rehearsal. Sticks and Quick is laughing it up about something.

"What's so funny man", I ask them. Sticks tells me that Quick is a Finger Zinger. I ask him what the hell a finger zinger is. He tells me that it means when someone's fingers are super fast. I tell him yhea man. He can play the shit out of that guitar. Sticks says man, you should have seen him with his fingers in Lil Mama. He was flicking his finger so fast inside her pussy; she was nutting all over the place. Begging him to stop and you know Lil Mama never says stop to no one-no body. We all start cracking up hysterically out loud.

The rest of the fellas came in and we start to warm up with our rehearsal. A few minutes later, Sticks says "Alright".

"Now let's get serious".

"Let's go over the new tune".

"The closer I get to you".

"But lets put a twist on it" he says.

"Alright yall, try to keep up". He counts the song off faster than anyone is used to. And we all come in and play together and it really sounds nice faster. Left starts some walking and popping the notes. Quick starts some kind of really nice sounding add libs. And Keys starts to overlay chords and strings together. I could not help but to join in with some super nice smokin runs. We really had something going on here.

We went through the song list a couple of times and we were solid. We are ready for the upcoming show.

So after rehearsal I went home and called Sexy. "Hey Sexy, how are you". I ask her.

She says "Hi Good. I'm fine what's up"?

I answer, "Oh, nothing much".

"I just got home from a cool rehearsal".

"Why you didn't show up"? She tells me that she had something to do and she couldn't make it. I sense that something is wrong and I ask her "Are you sure that there is nothing wrong"?

She tells me yhea im sure. Then I ask her if I can come over knowing that she was going to say no already. She says no just as I thought. Then she goes on to tell me that she is busy. So I tell her ok, I understand. I tell her goodbye and to have a goodnight. I hang up the phone and call up Baby.

The phone rings and she picks up. I greet her "Hey Baby, how you doing"?

She answers, "Hi Good. I'm fine. How are you"?

"I'm much better now baby". I answer her.

I go on to tell her how much I need her. "You know I need to see you baby. I am in need of your lovin baby". She tells me that tonight is not a good time she has to get up very early for a very important meeting.

Then she tells me that maybe I can come see her at lunch time tomorrow. I tell her great, I will call you before lunch time tomorrow. She tells me ok and to have a goodnight. I tell her that I will be thinking about her all night and I can't wait to see her tomorrow. She says that she can't make me any promises but call her and we will see if I can come by her job. I tell her ok sweetheart, you have a goodnight and sweet dreams. She tells me sweet dreams and we both hang up.

I get ready for bed and lay down for a moment before I fall asleep. I call up Tangy and talk to her awhile about how much I enjoy her company and I would love to see her again. She tells me that she really enjoys my company also and that she wants me to know that she really does like me a lot. I tell her that I really like her a lot too and I want her to be my lady.

She asks me if I am ready for that. I tell her that yes I am ready but I do have to cut some ties. I don't want anything or anyone to affect our relationship. She says you better get it together because I aint going to take no mess from you or your friends. I tell her that I really appreciate her being so understanding. She says to me that as long as we go into our relationship knowing what we have, then we shouldn't have any problems, right?

I tell her that that's absolutely right. I go on to tell her that I wish she was over here lying beside me. And she tells me that she wants it just like I do. I ask her what time does she have to be at school in the morning and she tells me that class doesn't start till eight a.m.

I ask her if she wants to come and spend the night and she says that we can't do anything, but I think that she is just testing me. So I tell her sure, we don't have to do anything. I just want you close to me.

She says that she will be right over and she will spend the night. I tell her that I will be waiting for her. She says don't you fall asleep on me, give me fifteen minutes. I tell her that I will be waiting. We hang up the phones and I lay back and fantasize about her.

A while later the phone rings and she says that she is in the front and I tell her that I will open the door. I get up and open the door she comes up to the door dressed in a long trench coat. I let her in and shut the door behind her. She stands there looking at me and I ask her, "What you have on your pajamas" anxiously waiting to see what's under the coat.

She opens the coat and she has on some very sexy lingerie. She asks me if I like what I see and I tell her I like it very much. I walk up to her and grab her coat for her and take it to the chair. I tell her to come let's go to bed. She looks at me as if she is a little puzzled because I didn't attack her. I get into bed and tell her to come get under the covers.

She climbs into the bed and I tell her to scoot over next to me and I hold her. I could not help but to get an erection but I try to play it cool. She tells me "Oh, looks like someone is not sleepy at all". I tell her that I'm sorry but he has a mind of his own.

I lean over to her, give her a kiss on the cheek and tell her "Goodnight my love".

She tells me goodnight baby and I turn off the TV. I lay there beside her for a moment and she backs that ass up on me and grinds her butt on me. I try not to move but I have a really hard erection as she knows it by moving her ass up and down on my dick. I tell her that if she keeps that up I will never go down from an erection.

She tells me that she is sorry but she likes my hard dick against her soft ass. I tell her that she has to stop if we are going to get any sleep tonight. She reaches over around behind her and grabs my hard erect penis. I couldn't help but to give her a moan because it felt so good. "Oooohhhh, baby".

She rubs it onto her ass crack up and down and then she gives me a welcoming sound. "Mmmmmmm that feels good" she says. She pulls my dick out of the opening of the front of my underwear and rubs it in her wet opening. Then she tells me "You see how wet I am for you daddy".

I tell her "yhea baby, you are so wet and I am so hard. I don't think we are going to get any sleep. She lifts her leg up and puts it around me as she guides my hard dick inside of her warm wet vagina. I slide right inside her and tell her that it feels so good as she throws her ass back at me.

"Oooohhh, that feels so good baby" I tell her again and again. She takes her hand from around my penis and grabs my ass cheek. "Give it to me Good" she says. "Give me all of you".

I stroke her slow and long. All the way in and all the way out as I grab her by the waist. We exchange yes sounds with each other for a few minutes and then I tell her to take off her clothes and she tells me that it unsnaps.

So she unsnaps it at the crotch. I the climb on top of her and look her in the eyes. I pull up one of her legs and she brings up the other willingly. I lean over and kiss her in her wet warm mouth and she sucks my tongue as we kiss.

I gently slide my dick back into her slippery tight pussy, giving her my "oooooh baby" once more. I grab her thigh as I stroke her slowly. In and out, repeatedly.

She starts to moan and groan and so do I. we share yes sounds together as I caress her legs and ass. She tells me that I'm driving her crazy as I suck on her neck and tickle her with my tongue. She moans louder and louder as she humps back at me. She tells me that she is going to cum and I tell her me too baby. We both get louder and start to stoke each other faster and faster.

"Yes, Yes baby" she tells me.

"Yhea, Yhea baby" I tell her. I give her my mercy humps harder and harder and she screams for more.

"Uh huh, Uh huh" she yells. "Oh my God, Oh...

I pound her wet pussy hard as I can just before I cum. Then I pull out and shoot my nut all over her stomach and up to her breast. I kneel there looking at her as I jack off and shoot my nut all over her stomach. She tells me oh baby as she rubs it into her skin. She puts one of her hands under my balls and gently caresses them.

She rubs my nut on her stomach and I fall down beside her and we lay there holding each other. Stroking and caressing each other, we come down together off of a sexual high. She tells me that she thinks that she is falling for me and I tell her I know exactly what she means.

She asks me "does that mean that I am falling for her too". I tell her "that is exactly what that means".

We kiss and she jumps up and goes into the bathroom and I hear the water turn on. She comes back out with a towel and wipes my dick off. The towel is warm and I tell her to be gentle with it. She tells me that she knows and I don't have to worry.

"Look baby, we both know what we want and I don't think that were hiding anything from one another so do you think that we should maybe one day soon move in with each other"?

She looks at me and laughs. "You know that is exactly what I was thinking too". I look into her eyes and say, "Now don't go jumping the gun. This aint gonna happen tomorrow".

She says "I know, but now we have something to look forward to". She gets up and goes into the bathroom to put the towel up.

When she comes back I tell her "Come here my baby". "Lay right here next to daddy".

She climbs into bed and scoots over beside me. I put one arm under her head and hold her with the other arm and she puts her arm around mine.

I tell her "Tangy, no matter what happens from here on, you are going to be my girl". She tells me "And you're going to be my man daddy". I tell her goodnight and give her a kiss. She says "Goodnight baby". We lay there holding one another as we both fall asleep.

The sun rises up and the birds are singing. I open my eyes and look at what I think is the most beautiful girl in the world. "Tangy baby" I whisper softly into her ear.

She opens her eyes and I tell her "Good morning sweetheart".

She answers back "Good morning baby".

I slide my arm from around her and tell her that I have to get ready for work but she can sleep if she wants to. She tells me "no that's ok, I will get up". We both jump up and get out of the bed.

"We slept well didn't we" I ask her. She says "Yes, we sure did".

"Damn Good"! "You sure know how to show a girl a good time. You put me right to sleep".

I tell her "Now you know why they call me Mr. Goodnight". She replies, "Oh really, I'm scared of you Mr. Goodnight".

Chapter Fifteen

I go into the bathroom and tell her "I hope that you really like me because what I'm about to do in here could break up the average marriage". She laughs and says "You stank that bad".

I tell her "You may want to leave while you have a chance". She hands me the spray and tells me you better spray in there. I close the bathroom door and start to make some grunting sounds. Uuuuuuhhhh, uuuuuhhhhh. She starts cracking up out loud. Then she tells me to let her know if she needs to dial the last one. She already has nine and one pressed.

I give her a courtesy flush so it doesn't smell so bad. Then when I finish I wipe and flush. I start to spray as I open the door and ask her "Please don't go in there for about thirty to forty minutes". She tells me "That spray aint helping you know, I could still smell it from under the door and you stink".

"So how am I supposed to go inside there after you went in there and did that"? I laugh at her and tell her you know we sound like were married already. She tells me "Well if that is what I have to look forward to I don't want to get married". And we both start cracking up laughing.

I finish getting ready for work and she gets ready also. So before I leave for work I tell her that I really had a great time last night and I am glad that she came by and spent the night with me. She says that she also had a great time and we should do it again. I agree with her.

I open the door and turn to her to give her a great big hug and kiss. She hugs me back tightly and I get a big squeeze of her ass. We kiss a few times and we say our goodbyes. I tell her that I will call her later and she says ok as she walks in a different direction than me.

I get in my car and drive off to work. I don't even call anyone on my way to work.

I get to work and it's a usual day for me. I remember that I told Baby that I would maybe come by for lunch but it was already lunch time so I don't call her. Instead, I call up Lil Mama.

Ring, ring. "Hello" she answers.

I speak, "What's up Lil Mama, how you doin"?

She says "Good, what's happening with you man? You gone invite me over for the football game again this weekend"?

I tell her maybe, but I may be busy this weekend. I have something to ask you. She says "Oh boy, here we go. Every time you got something to ask me it's always not good".

I laugh a little and say "You ready for this"? She says "Go ahead, what is it"?

I say, "I think I'm in love". She starts laughing really loud and puts the phone down as she cracks up in the background.

I say "Lil Mama", but no answer.

"Lil Mama", I repeat but no answer.

She comes back to the phone and says "Negro Please".

"What's her name"?

I tell her that her name is Tangy.

She says "I know you wasn't going to say that bitch that came over the other day while I was there".

I tell her "No, you haven't met this one yet". "Maybe you will get a chance to meet her one day". She asks me if I really like her and I tell her yes, I do.

She asks me if we have had sex yet and I tell her yes, of course we have.

She ask me if she can suck a good dick and I tell her that she doesn't have to worry, no body sucks a good dick like she does. She tells me "well I don't see how you in love with her ass then".

I tell her that every time I think about her I get a warm feelin inside. She keeps me satisfied and we have fun together. I can talk to her about anything and she is very understanding. Lil Mama says "she sounds like a very nice lady".

I tell her that she is a lady in the street and a freak in the bed. So Lil Mama is quiet for a moment and then she tells me to just give it some time and let what ever is going to happen, happen.

I tell her that I will and that she is still my special friend. Nobody or no one will ever change that. She says "Good, that's why I like you, because you always keep it one hundred with me. Then she tells me if I really like her to treat her right and don't be fuckin around on her like I do with all those other bitches.

I tell her that she is right and I have been thinking about that already. I just don't know how to tell them that I have a girl. She tells me that I will and don't worry about it. I say thanks for being there for me and she says its nothing. We say our goodbyes and hang up.

I go back to work and the time passes so fast that I didn't get a chance to call anyone. So after work, I head for Sticks place just to talk with him. We don't have rehearsal today but he is on the way home anyway.

I get to Sticks spot, go inside and nock on the door. He opens the door and says, "What's up Daddy-o"?

I tell him nothing, just came by to kick some shit with you.

He says, "I can dig it, come on in baby".

I enter inside Sticks spot and he's got some cool shit bumpin with a bad ass drummer on it. So man, he says. "Whats cookin"?

I tell him that he knows me and we been friends for a long time. He says "Yhea". I'm just gone skip the bull shit and get right to the point.

He says "Yhea". I tell him that I think that I'm in love and he says "Yhea". I go on to say that I met a lady and she makes me feel like I never felt before. I always think about her and she keeps a smile on my face.

He says "Yhea". I tell him "Come on man, I'm serious".

He tells me "You were serious about 5 other times before and were did it get you man".

"All you did was pop your top. You got to remember that it is always good in the beginning. Then after awhile, you start to see things clearer and clearer. I'm not in no way trying to stop you from doing whatever you want to do, but I just want you to know that a real relationship you have to work at. It's not going to be easy all the time. Look at you Good. You're a player man. Players play all day and some. Are you really ready to give it all up for some chick"?

I look at him and think about it. He goes on and tells me "Here today gone tomorrow".

"If you are ready you better make sure that she got something other than a fine ass body. Once her fine ass body goes and then what you got left"?

I tell him that maybe I just need a little vacation from all the bitches.

"I feel like I am missing something inside. Something that only real love can give me. I don't love those hoes. I just love em and leave em. This lady I feel like I can really love. I can really spend some time with her". I don't have to lie to her and she understands me. We laugh and joke all the time and I aint even talking about sex yet. Its like she makes love to my mind, my heart and my body. She got me sprung man. I thought I would never say that. But I think it might be true".

Sticks start busting up, laughing at me and says, "Man I know you aint pussy whipped". So I tell him "Man it aint even like that. I guess I'm getting a little older or wiser or something. I got busted at the hair shop the other day and I must be slippin because I never get caught up. But I saw her and lost it. I acted on some shit like I never done before. I thought about her and not me".

Sticks tells me, "You must be on some love shit then".

"Just be careful my brotha".

"All is fair in love and war. I know you heard that shit before".

I tell him "Yhea, I heard that before".

"Well usually after we talk like this I would tell you Pimps up and Hoes down, But this is some way out there shit man".

"Am I supposed to give you a hug or something? Man, I think we need to write a song or something so we can wax a disc. We can call it "Send". I tell him "alright that's a bet".

"Alright man then I will see you later man".

He tells me "All right Daddy-o".

"Peace out Sticks", I tell him and I split to the pad.

When I get home, I start to think about all of the women that I had been with. I start going down the list and asking myself if I was going to continue on with them or give them up for Tangy. So let's see.

Sexy - She gave me the ass and she can sing her ass off. Hmm, don't know.

Baby - I really like her. She is extremely beautiful and daring. Although she is kinda hard to get next to. I don't know.

Lil Mama - She will always be my friend and I just won't have a sexual relationship with her anymore. Man, that's going to be very difficult,

Denise – Not a problem, I haven't done anything with her yet. No love lost.

Alize – I don't really like her that much. She likes drama and I don't see a future for us as girlfriend and boyfriend.

Well that settles it. I guess I am ready to give them all up for Tangy.

Let me see. Tangy – she's very understanding. Honest. She's easy to get along with. Accepts me for who I am. She makes good love to me. She supports me and my music. And I don't think that she will cheat on me.

She's everything that I need and want in a woman. I guess that settles it. I know what I want and now all I have to do is make it happen.

I call up Sexy. She answers the phone. "Hello Good. How are you"?

I tell her that I'm fine but I have some bad news. She says "What is it? I tell her that I am seeing someone else and I think it is getting serious.

She tells me "That's ok Good. I know about all your friends and lovers".

I say to her, "You do"? She replies, "Yes I do".

"I knew exactly what I was getting into with you when we first started out".

"Don't worry", she says, "I am still your friend".

I tell her "Thanks for understanding and being cool about it".

I tell her that I will see her later on and she tells me "Ok sweetheart, Goodnight".

I tell her goodnight and we hang up.

I think to myself this might be easier than I thought. I call up Baby. The phone rings and she answers.   "Hello", she says.

"Hi Baby, its Good".

She answers, "Hi Good". "How you doing"?

I tell her I'm doing fine but I have some bad news. She says what is it. I ask her if she's sitting down and she tells me yhea, I'm sitting down.

I tell her that I really like her a lot so I'm just going to come out and say it. She says what is it Good.

I tell her that I seeing someone and I really don't want to hurt anyone so I wanted you to know that before it got any more serious. She tells me that it's ok and she understands. She goes on to say that she was just using me anyway. She is too busy for a regular relationship and I was just someone that was easy to have.

I kinda felt like she purposely used me and the shoes were on the other foot. But that's what you get when you think you got it going on. I tell her "So now that we both got our dirt out, can we still be friends"?

She tells me sure. "I'm sorry that it had to come to this but we had some fun didn't we".

I tell her "Yes, we did have some fun though". "So I guess I will see you around then", I tell her.

She says "Alright Good", "I guess we will see each other around". And we both hang up.

Then I call up Alize. The phone rings and she answers. "Hello"?

"Hello there Alize, how are you"? I ask her.

She says that she is fine and ask me how am I doing? I tell her that I'm good but I have to talk to her about something. She says what is it. So I tell her that I don't think that we should see each other again and she tells me "Why, it's that bitch that I saw you with aint it".

I tell her "You know I have to be honest with you. It does have something to do with her but it's you too. I am getting serious with her but you have issues of your own".

She cuts me off and says "What do you mean I got issues. I gave in to you and this is how you treat me. I should have never slept with your ass in the first place. That's what's wrong with men today, all they want is a piece of ass and then they can't even keep that. You go on with that bitch and I hope that she makes you happy. Y'all probably deserve each other anyway".

I tell her that we can still be friends and I will never forget her.

She tells me "Friends, I don't think so. Friends don't treat friends like you treated me".

I cut her off and say "Well you never were my girlfriend anyway. We were just someone that met at your job and had a good time together".

Then she calms down and says "Well you know I did like your gumbo and you did show me a good time".

I tell her that I had a great time with her too. Then she says "Well, if she doesn't treat you right you have my number, call me".

I tell her "Ok, I will". And I go on to say "I will see you at work when I do my shopping". She says "Ok Good. You have a goodnight".

I tell her "Goodnight" and we both hang up our phones.

I sit there for a while and then I call Tangy up. The phone rings and she picks up. "Hello" she says.

I answer, "Hi Tangy". "How are you"?

"I have something really important to tell you but I want to tell you face to face". Can you come over for a moment please? She says "sure, I will be right over".

We hang up and a few minutes later she knocks on the door. I go to the door to answer it. I open the door and there she is. The most beautiful woman I ever laid eyes on. Hi Tangy, come on in I tell her. She comes inside and I show her to the couch.

"Have a seat baby" I tell her. She sits down and I sit right beside her. I take her hand and say "Where do I start".

I start to mumble about how a man needs a woman by his side and that sometimes a man has to choose his paths. Then I look at her and tell her. "I'm just going to come out and say it. I want you to be my lady. I have gotten rid of all my friends and told them that I was not going to be able to see them anymore. If it is alright with you, I want us to be together as a couple".

She looks at me and says "sure I will be your lady".

We give each other a big hug and kiss on it. She tells me "I didn't think that you were going to do it".

"I know that it was a big thing for you but I'm glad you did it".

Chapter Sixteen

I tell her that I really like you a lot and I want us to be together. She gets up and grabs my hand and tells me "let me show you how much I appreciate this".

She pulls me up from the couch and leads me into the bedroom. Stands me beside the bed and kisses me on the lips. I kiss her back and we both go into a slow, long and wet passionate French kiss.

She moans letting me know that she loves it and I moan back to let her know that I am also getting excited.

She starts to unbutton my shirt and I start to take of hers. We are both pulling each others clothes off and I start to move down her neck, kissing her slowly and licking her neck. She tells me "Take me Good, I'm yours".

I unfasten her bra and caress her soft tender breast. I hold one of her breast and look at it before I lick it slowly. Then I kiss it and suck it gently, squeezing it softly and then firmly. She sighs as I squeeze firmly, letting me know that she loves every moment of it.

I change breast and lick, suck and squeeze the same as the first one. She tells me "Oh, Good. That feels so good". I start to pull her pants off by unfastening them. She starts to unbuckle my pants. Then we both stop and start to undress ourselves. I take off my pants and underwear and throw them onto the chair. She slides her pants and panties off and puts them on the edge of the bed.

We walk to each other and she tells me "Now, let me show you how much I appreciate how my man was man enough to do the right thing".

She tells me to sit down, so I do. Then she tells me to lie back, so I do. She climbs on top of me and starts to kiss me in the mouth. I kiss her back and she goes down to my neck. Then she kisses me on the chest and stomach next. She grabs my dick with one hand and say's "Oooohhhh, is that for me"?

I tell her "Yes baby, that's your hard dick".

She starts to lick it up and down. Then she licks around the head. I tell her "that's right baby, sharpen the tool before we use it".

After licking on it for a little while she puts it inside her warm mouth. "OOhhhh that feels so good baby" I tell her.

First she starts slow and then she speeds up a little faster. I tell her to go slow baby. It feels much better when you go slowly. "Mmmmmm that feels so good baby" I tell her as she slows down.

She cups her hand under my balls and holds them. Oh it feels so good and she knows it. My dick is so hard that I want her now and badly too. I tell her "Tangy, I want you baby".

She says OK baby, just a minute. Then she starts stroking my dick as she sucks it and moves her head in a circular motion. This is driving me crazy and she can tell because I am making all kind of ooh's and aah's and jerking and squirming.

I tell her that "Damn, that feels so good baby". And before I knew it I almost came, but it was like she knew and stopped just before I came. Then she gets on top of me and slides my hard erect penis inside of her warm wet pussy.

My dick was so hard that it slid in with no problem. And we both moan together. "Oohh".

Then we start to fuck each other. I hump her and she humps me back. I stop as to let her get her nut and she rides me like the long ranger. Changing strides on the dick, up and down first, then front to back.

She is working me like crazy. Pounding her ass on top of me as she squats over me, she starts to give me those yes sounds and I can feel she is gong to climax.

Shit, she is working the dick so good that I am also going to cum. So I start to pound back and we both get louder and louder with the ooh's and ahs. She gets even louder and says "Fuck me Good, Fuck meeeee".

I start to give it to her real good from under her, but the pussy is so hot and tight that I know I'm going to cum. She screams louder as she can feel my dick get harder and larger as all the blood goes to the head of my dick. I grab her ass and she grabs mine as we scream together in ecstasy. "Yhea, Yhea baby, Yhea, I'm cumming, Me tooooo".

She locks up and I give her my last couple of mercy humps. Then we both lay there together, me still inside of her and her still on top of me. I can feel her pussy throbbing around my dick and she can feel my dick throbbing inside of her as I ejaculate all inside her hot pussy. I think to myself, if we keep this up we are surly going to have a baby.

I caress her and she rubs on me as we both are flying high in the clouds on cloud nine. I can honestly say that I never knew love like this before.

THE END